HOLD ZERO!

HOLD
ZERO!

BY JEAN CRAIGHEAD GEORGE

Thomas Y. Crowell Company

New York

TO JOAN GORDON
*who knows what it is
to be herself.*

CONTENTS

HOLD
ZERO!

1 CRAIG

"And now," said Steve Jungkatz, "it's T-minus sixty minutes and holding for the final countdown. Let's go home and eat."

Craig Sutton heard the excitement in his friend's voice and it sent a shiver down his own back. He glanced at the rocket gleaming above the launching pit and felt his heart shake his body. It was done, every detail was complete, and in one hour the months of work that the four boys—he and Steve, and Johnny Cooper and Phil Brundage—had put into the construction of the rocket would be rewarded by a roaring, fiery spectacle above the island in the marsh of Blue Springs, New York. The day, Saturday, September 24, was warm and green and filled with expectation.

Craig stepped out of the launch pit and followed Steve through the hemlocks and willows to the wharf at the south end of the island. Johnny hurried ahead of Steve, clicking his heels at every third step. Craig laughed and leaped for a limb. It dipped and crackled and its leaves, he thought, clanged and rang out. Suddenly he realized Phil was not close behind. He turned to see him dragging along in the moody silence that had taken hold of him for the past week.

"Come on!" Craig shouted exuberantly and swung his whole arm and body in a beckon.

Phil looked up, said, "Huh?" and plodded forward as if his legs were hard to move. "Yeah," he added and regained his outward enthusiasm. He joined the other boys at the wharf but sat silent when the swamp buggy, with its homemade paddle wheel and steering gear, moved laboriously out into the broad shallow lake. Craig ignored him and joined in the excited conversation with Johnny and Steve, who was fifteen—two years his senior.

At the second wharf, hidden in the reeds on the town side of the big marsh, Craig tied up the swamp buggy, then sprinted up the hill calling, "See ya in an hour." He heard his friends repeat his words like crows sending assembly calls through their ranks.

He chuckled to himself and climbed up the steep hill to his brown shingle house on the ridge. He passed the Olsens' house and called to Mr. Olsen who was doggedly using this Saturday to rake the first of the falling leaves from his wide green lawn. For a moment Craig felt an impulse to shout, "A rocket will be launched in one hour," but the secret had been kept too long to share it now.

He went up the stone steps and walked into the vestibule where the fountain his mother had made trickled softly over the rocks and plunged into a wide pool. He glanced at his sister's guitar on the piano, felt his excitement return, and went into the kitchen where his mother was making sandwiches.

"Hi!" he said, and his voice belled so loudly she turned and looked at him.

"Oh, hi," she said. "Hurry up and eat, I have to go to a meeting."

Craig paid no attention. Meetings and discussion groups and community activities were so much a part of his mother's life since she and his father had been divorced that he would have been surprised if she were *not* working on some plan to better the school and the social activities of the Blue Springs children.

His sister Ellen and his younger brother Pete scuffed to their chairs and sat down. They were arguing over whether Carl Mants was a "dope" or a "hero," and Craig quickly stopped listening because he didn't care. He turned his mind to the rocket, with its microclips and engines, waiting for the final countdown. He hoped the booster engines would glow red, as the catalogue said they would.

Suddenly the telephone rang. Craig's mother picked it up. "Yes, it is." she said. She sounded worried. A barrage of words from a male voice carried all the way across the table. "Yes, indeed, come right over," she said and hung up. She stared at Craig. "Mr. Brundage has reported to the police that you and Steve and Johnny and Phil have made a rocket. A policeman wants to talk to you."

Craig rose to his feet in shock. "Oh," he said. "I'll go get Steve." He swallowed a dry bite as he realized what had been bothering Phil. Apparently he had decided he had to tell his father about the rocket.

Craig took a few steps toward the door, then

came back. "It's perfectly safe," he said to his mother.

Her eyes had widened with astonishment. "But," she stammered, "when have you had time to make a rocket?"

Craig ignored her and ran out the front door. He paused on the steps and shoved his hands into his pockets. The tops of the trees were just beginning to change from green to gold, and the blackbirds were clustering aimlessly in the color as if the idea of migration were vaguely occurring to them. "Poor Phil," he said and jumped down the entire bank of stairs to the path. He ran. Halfway up the hill he took the path through the hedge of forsythia that led to Steve's house. Its steep gables, its white trim went unnoticed. All he saw was the second-floor window and Steve's head bent over, reading.

"Pheee!" Craig whistled. No answer. He moistened his lips and discovered his tongue was dry. He tried to whistle again. The window opened, and Steve, a dark-haired boy with strong cheekbones that shadowed his face, leaned out and grinned. "Whatdayawant?" he called. "It's still early. Is something wrong?"

Craig nodded.

"Why didn't you call on the transceiver?"

Steve yelled down. Craig gestured helplessly.

"Is it *that* bad?"

Craig nodded again. Steven slammed the window shut.

In moments Craig heard Steve's size-ten sneakers staccato down the steps and pound the kitchen floor. Craig watched him vault over the back porch railing and run toward him.

"A cop's on the way to the house to see about the rocket," Craig said. "Phil told his dad, and his dad reported it."

Steve whistled softly. "I guess we'd better get Johnny," he said.

"We can't. He's practicin' the piano now."

"Oh, yeah." Steve ran his fingers through his hair. "Well, this is a crisis!" he said. "He'll have to use the tape recorder."

Craig laughed, and the thought of using the tape recorder to get Johnny out of practicing lightened his mind. "He's even got a new reel. He made it last week." He grabbed Steve's arm and started down the hill to the road that bordered the marsh and wound northward toward Johnny's house.

Craig and Steve followed the road, edged with pokeweed and Queen Anne's lace, until they came to a path that wound through the red maples. They plunged between the water willows and viburnum and into the woods as they circled the marsh on the shortcut to Johnny's side of town. Craig picked a leaf and twirled it.

"That Johnny!" he said. "He recorded *La Bohème* all the way through last week. Didn't even stop for rests. Said his mother couldn't tell the difference as long as the music kept coming." Steve chuckled. Then plaintively, Craig added, "Mrs. Cooper really keeps Johnny busy with projects that are good for him, doesn't she?"

"Yep," Steve agreed. "But it doesn't bother Johnny. He's a thinker. Plans himself out of things." Steve jumped for a wild grape leaf. "The tape machine is great," he went on, "but, you know, he works harder making those tapes than all the practicing anyone could force on him."

"And he's got a stand-in for dancing class," Craig added. "Fred'll come take his place anytime Johnny wants to go fishin'!"

"Yeah," said Steve enviously, "and remember how he got out of the Togetherness Picnic? I was jealous of that for a month."

"Gee." Craig laughed at the memory. "He hid in that panel truck that brought the box lunches. We hadda run relay races with our folks." Steve broke into laughter. "And then," Craig went on, "the darn truck took off and drove on to Yankee Stadium, went in the service entrance, and Johnny saw the whole game from the back of the truck. And I was back at the picnic trying not to be embarrassed when my mother picked up the bat and played baseball." Craig thought about it. "It was awful. Ruined our 'togetherness' for a month."

"They shouldn't have those things," Steve said firmly. "I can't understand what they think we get out of it. A guy doesn't want to see his mother playing baseball like a kid. He wants her to be—" he hesitated, "an adult. Fathers too. When my father lived with us he always felt he had to hack around with me. It made me nervous. I always felt he was forcing himself to act like a boy."

They had circled the marsh and were making their way uphill through tulip poplars and gray birch when they heard the sounds of Johnny practicing. On hands and feet they stole across the Coopers' yard and crept into the rhododendron bushes that grew around the yellow clapboard house. Craig led the way to the windows of the "fun room." He peered under the bamboo blinds. Johnny was playing painfully.

"Pssssssst," Craig called. The piano stopped almost immediately—as Craig knew it would —for Johnny was keenly attuned to outside diversions with every note he played. He came to the door and opened it.

"Hi!" he whispered. "I can't come yet. It's not one o'clock."

"We got a crisis," Steve whispered.

"Yeah?"

"Phil told his dad about the rocket, and his dad called the police. A cop is on his way to Craig's house now to see what we're doing."

"Wow!" whispered Johnny.

Steve rasped impatiently, "Put on the tape recorder and let's go. This is an emergency." Craig whirled through the door as Johnny glanced at his mother in the living room.

"She's still talking to that PTA woman about wholesome parties for the school," he whispered. "The tape's in the piano seat. Get it, Craig. I'll keep playing while you all set up the machine."

With the air of a man saved from the gallows Johnny went back to the piano and sprang upon the keys. The two women in the other room stopped talking. Johnny played louder. The voices started up again, and Craig deftly put the tape on the spindles and threaded it into the machine. Steve plugged in the cord and turned on the switch.

Two concerts bellowed out: Johnny on the tape and Johnny at the keys. Craig gasped, and

Steve grabbed for the volume button. He adjusted the noise as Johnny lifted his fingers and let the tape play on. He peered once more at his mother and signaled his friends to ease out the door.

Craig did not glance back as he followed Steve and Johnny across the lawn and into the brush behind a hill of tumbled boulders.

"It's a good thing Mom's no musician," he heard Johnny say as he slid into the wild geraniums. "A four-handed solo and she never turns her head." Craig was under the ground cover now. A crane fly winged over the geraniums toward his face. The insect sensed his presence, veered to the left, and skimmed over the head of a motionless wood thrush. Without ceremony the bird reached up and swallowed the fly, then settled back, its bright eye focused on the boys. Craig watched the bird without thinking about it.

"Are we gonna get Phil?" Johnny asked.

"Aw, let's leave him alone," Craig said. "He must feel pretty awful."

"His dad never has liked rockets," Steve put in. "Phil told me once his father was on a committee to protect kids from certain fuel mixtures. It must be hard to be a minister's son."

Craig whistled softly to the wood thrush,

then followed his friends downhill. He saw Steve struggling with the reeds and stepped ahead to help him. "Thanks, brother nature," Steve teased. "Go first, I can't find the durn trail."

Craig found it and let Steve pass. He waited for Johnnny. Johnny wove with loose movements among the leathery alders and the grasping Phragmites reeds. Craig's admiration for him welled up. "Can'tcha get us out of this?" Craig pleaded as Johnny drew up. "You always get us out of messes." Mosquitoes whined as the boys knocked against the bushes, and Craig swung at them.

"There are times when you put your back to the music in order to face it," Johnny said. "There's no way out."

"Yeah," Craig took a deep breath, "but cops —gee, they spell trouble." He hiked his trousers to steady his nerves. Through the copper stems of the river birches he saw the gray softness of the marsh.

"Are we going to tell them about Batta?" he asked. Johnny and Steve slowed down, and the three boys looked at each other in distress. Steve's dark eyebrows puckered, then lifted. "No," he said firmly. "That's our secret. It's got nothing to do with the rocket."

"Right," echoed Johnny. "Let's shake." He shoved one hand into Craig's, the other into Steve's, and Craig felt better.

"What about the door from the launching pit to Batta?" Steve called as they hurried on. "If we have to show the cop the rocket and the launch pit, he'll surely ask about the door."

"We'd better cover it with mud bags," Johnny suggested.

"Good idea," Steve agreed. "But we'll have to move the command station. We'll have to move the ignition control panel and the intercom system from Batta."

"Put them in the fire control bunker," suggested Craig. "We'll make that the command center."

"Good," said Steve.

"Suppose the cop wants to see the rocket this afternoon?" Craig asked.

"Well, we'll have to stall him—till we change things," Johnny said. "There's always something we can say we have to do—scouts, orchestra, Little League, dancing, geezey, we've got enough to do without faking a single excuse."

They were almost to the road. Craig wasn't ready to see the policeman, and began to slow the pace. Finally he stopped.

"Whatya lookin' at?" Johnny asked.

"The muskrat den," Craig said. "The entrance's closed with leaves. Do you suppose they're all right?"

"Oh, frogs eggs, Craig!" Steve said irritably when he saw the brown shapeless dome in the reeds. "Here you are worrying about a muskrat den when you should be planning the new layout of gear in the fire control station." His voice was sharp, but Craig noticed he stood a long time staring at the den and the sticks and leaves jutting from the waterline door.

They moved on, crossed Rushing Road, climbed Hobbs Drive, and turned down the lane that led to Craig's house. They stopped. A white police car, red light flashing ominously, sat in front of the brown shingle house.

"Well," Johnny said finally, "here goes nothin'."

As Craig plunged forward, he noticed his legs were stiff at the knees. But he climbed the steps resolutely and slowly pulled back the screen door.

2 OFFICER RICARDO

Craig watched his mother introduce Steve and Johnny to Police Officer Ricardo. Then she gave his name—rather stiffly, he thought—and he realized she was nervous. He tried to sense what she was thinking, but the officer absorbed his interest. He had a broad thick chest, black hair graying at the edges, and heavy brows that shadowed his eyes. As he got up to meet them Craig wondered whether the man's head was

going to bump the red ceiling his mother so prized. He had never seen so tall a man.

"Now!" The officer's voice was a boom on the bass drum. "What's all this about a rocket?"

The boys found chairs and sat down. Craig glanced at Steve who licked his lips but did not answer.

"What've ya made?" the officer asked. His smile seemed condescending. "One of those CO_2 cartridges with match heads stuck in it?"

"No, sir." Steve was annoyed. "It's a three-stage booster." The officer laughed boyishly and Craig shifted his feet.

"Of course, you know there's a law against putting off rockets," the officer said.

"It's still pending. Hasn't been passed yet," Craig whispered.

"But there *is* a law against incendiaries." Johnny spoke up from the straight-backed chair in the corner.

The officer cleared his throat. "You seem to know the rules. Don't you know you're supposed to get permission to set off a rocket?"

"Yes, sir," Steve said.

"Why didn't you?"

"We didn't think anyone would know any more about them than we do, and so we didn't bother," Steve replied.

Craig glanced down at his shoes and then up to see how the officer was taking Steve's answer. Craig almost smiled when he saw the man's face—his eyebrows were trembling, and he seemed to be trying to decide whether to be shocked or angry.

"What makes you think the police staff hasn't had this kind of problem before?" the officer finally asked. "I took the Rogers boy to the police firing range to put off one he'd made. Now, we could've done this for you." His voice was firm. "Why didn't you call? You know the rules."

"This isn't exactly a rocket you can put off on a firing range," Steve answered. "It's a three-stage booster with a remote control launching panel. Rules set up by the rocket clubs say you have to launch it electrically from behind a foot-thick barricade. I don't think we could do that at a rifle range."

"I see," said the officer, but his tone did not sound as if he saw at all. He laughed. "You boys today are great . . . launching panel. When I was a boy we had firecrackers. Put 'em under tin cans and sent them sky high." He twisted his head at pleasant but dangerous memories. "It's a wonder we weren't all killed. We didn't call them launching panels in our day. Didn't know the words. We just called them bombs."

Johnny said that must have been keen fun, and the conversation died.

Craig's mother came to the rescue. "It may be all right," she said brightly. "After all, they've made radios with little parts and pieces."

"Condensers and resistors," Steve explained.

Officer Ricardo slapped his knees together in pleasure, and Craig had the awful feeling that he was not taking them very seriously.

"Maybe you ought to come see what we've done," Craig suggested, somewhat surprised at his own calmness.

"Yes," his mother said. "Perhaps it's not as dangerous as we think. It may be quite good."

Another condescending pause.

"After all," she began again, "Mr. Diamond gave that radio kit to Craig—wires all hanging out—because *he* couldn't make it. Said he had bought it as a project so that he and his son might get to know each other better." She laughed. "He said the directions were absolutely unintelligible and that the whole thing had ended up in his being frustrated and angry at his son."

"You boys got it together?" asked the officer.

"Oh sure," answered Steve. "Craig and I talk on it all the time. Phil and Johnny are too far away for the FCC regulations. You see, we can only use a fifty-foot aerial or we'll interfere with other bands."

"I see," said Officer Ricardo.

"What I don't understand," Craig's mother broke in, "is why this whole rocket business started anyway. This town has everything to make a child happy. There are dancing classes, orchestras to play in, bands, soccer, football, Little League, Boy Scouts, choirs, drama groups, ski trips, ice skating . . . seems sort of silly to go off by yourselves and make rockets and radios when there is so much offered." She sighed.

"Frankly, Mrs. Sutton," Officer Ricardo said rather gently, "I don't know what the stir's about. So, some boys made a rocket. I'll tell you what I'll do. I'll have a look at it and get the chief to okay the whole thing. I'm sure he will." He rose. "Where is it, Steve?"

"On an island in the marsh."

"That sounds safe." The officer crossed his arms over his chest. "Maybe we can let you boys go ahead with it." He turned to Johnny, who had bounced to his feet happily.

"How high does it go? Thirty or forty feet?"

"Two thousand," Johnny answered.

"Two thousand?" Craig saw the officer's eyebrows lower ominously.

"Oh, now, Johnny," Mrs. Sutton said, "that's like a real rocket."

"It *is* a real rocket," Johnny replied.

The officer stepped toward the vestibule. "When can I see this? I'm busy this afternoon, but tomorrow morning I'm on duty in this area. Could we meet at eleven?"

"That would be fine," Steve said and glanced with relief at Craig. But Craig was looking at the officer's feet. They splayed out, he noticed.

Then the telephone rang. His mother stepped into the kitchen to answer it. She said a few "yeses," an "oh," and signaled the policeman to wait. She hung up and came into the vestibule. The falling water of the fountain sounded loud and steady.

"That was Mr. Brundage," she said. "Phil's father. He's terribly upset. His son told him that the rocket had twenty-four engines and was thirty-two inches tall—without the top on."

"The nose cone," Steve corrected.

"Yes, that's it." She went on, "Mr. Brundage said he thought a committee ought to be formed to check the rocket and see what's going on. He suggested you and himself, and Johnny's father, the town supervisor . . . and a scientist."

"Can they come tomorrow?" the officer asked.

"Oh, I doubt it. It's Sunday. Mr. Brundage will be tied up at the church and the others will be busy I'm sure. It'll have to be organized."

"Yes, organized," the officer repeated and Craig was reminded of the crows again. "Well, I'll go ahead. Perhaps a committee won't be necessary." The big man spun on his heel, then dropped a large hand on Mrs. Sutton's shoulder. "Don't worry," he said, "everything's going to be all right."

"It's just that Mr. Brundage is so upset that this got 'out of hand,'" she said hopelessly. "He can't understand how a rocket got built without adult supervision."

Craig was eager to correct his mother. "Oh, lots of adults helped," he said. "Mr. Brian, the science teacher, checked out the launch panel at school, and Mr. Pappo, that free-lance inventor, gave us lots of condensers and old tubes. Even Mr. Brundage helped Phil carve the first-stage nose cones out of balsa wood."

"You mean it *was* supervised?" Officer Ricardo said brightly.

"Well, not exactly." Johnny took up the explanation. "Everybody kind of helped us in their free time. But the funny thing was," he turned his head slightly, "nobody asked us what it was for. And we just sort of never told them. They were all so busy with their own work."

Craig watched Officer Ricardo's face as he scratched his head and put on his cap. He opened the door and hesitantly turned back to say something. But he was interrupted as Craig's brother Pete called loudly from the basement and his sister Ellen burst in the back door with a friend, crying, "Hey? who's being arrested?"

Officer Ricardo threw open the door. "See you all at eleven sharp. I'm getting curious about this Cape Kennedy of Blue Springs." But his laugh seemed forced.

Craig's watch read 1 P.M. He shook it, then stared at the small hand that had inexorably arrived at the numeral that not long ago was to be the most exciting number in his life—one.

"It's T-time," he said to Johnny and Steve, "and all systems are red." Johnny's eyes dampened as he turned away.

3 THE MARSH

Craig's mother came into his room after an early supper to tell him it was time to leave for the Community Night. He was lying on his bed, his math book spread open before him. He did not look up. "Zero, one, two, three, four," he said, "ten, eleven, twelve, thirteen, fourteen. Twenty, twenty-one . . ."

"What kind of counting is that?" she asked.

"New math. Base five." Craig lowered his

head. "Guess I shouldn't go to Community Night."

"It does sound as if it needs some work," she said. "Well, don't stay up late."

Craig stared at black numbers until the door closed softly and the sounds of his family's footsteps faded on the front steps. He repeated the numbers as he listened to the murmur of his transceiver, its switch opened to Steve's house. The disappointment of the afternoon was at last layered over with thoughts of the work ahead at Batta. He rolled on his back and bicycled in the air.

A loud sputter from his radio landed him on his feet on the floor. He turned up the volume.

"Steve to Craig! Steve to Craig!" the radio sputtered. "Do you read me? Over."

Craig flicked his button to "broadcast" and picked up a square gray microphone. "Craig to Steve. I read you go. Over."

The radio crackled. Steve's voice came in again. "Mom's gone. Are you ready? Let's meet at the swamp buggy in fifteen minutes. I'll stop by for Johnny. Better get some paint for the rocket. If it looks good I think Officer Ricardo will let us put it off. Don't you? Over."

"I dunno. Mr. Brundage still has to check it, and he's pretty strong-minded when he gets going. Over."

"Yeah. Well, we've gotta try. See ya. Out."

"Roger and out." Craig turned off the radio.

Fifteen minutes had brought the sun to the rim of the northern ridge of the great marsh. Craig crossed Rushing Road and disappeared into a tangle of willows. He found the path that led to the wharf the four boys had built, its pilings hammered into the mud, its flooring nailed carefully to a square frame. Craig jumped on the wharf that stood in a gray-green screen of Phragmites grass. Beyond, according to the depth of the water, grew hard-stem bulrushes and water lilies. Then the slow stream stretched out into a meandering lake that formed the basis of the marsh. It was a half-mile wide and three-quarters of a mile long.

Craig waited for John and Steve. He listened for the cracking of the bushes that would tell of their coming but heard only the arguments of the red-winged blackbirds settling on reeds and branches for the night. He snapped on his flashlight and lifted the plastic cover that protected the swamp buggy from the rain. He checked the gasoline in the old lawn mower engine that Mr. Olsen had given him and examined the paddle wheel that moved the craft. He remembered gathering the shingles for paddle blades when the Rovers renovated their house several years ago. But he was particularly proud of the iron hoops that held the blades. They had been taken from lobster barrels at the end of a neighborhood party. He stepped on the buggy and looked over the edge to see whether the oil drums that held the flat floor above the water were leaking. They seemed fine.

He filled the gas tank, then sat down to wait for the others. A soft click in the willows attracted his attention. "Hi, Squawker!" he said as he peered into the cobweb of limbs to locate the friendly blue jay that roosted there every evening. A soft spot among the stiff branches was all Craig could see of the bird. He squinted, moved closer and saw that the breast feathers were fluffed. The heckler of the marsh appeared gentle. Craig thrust his fist toward him, first and little fingers raised, so that his hand and wrist made the outline of an owl. He knew Squawky would object, because an owl's shape—live, dead, or badly imitated —made him angry. He could not help it; his mind was imprinted with hate for a round head and tufted ears. The bird screamed. Craig laughed and turned away.

He lay down on the wharf and shone his flashlight into the water. Small animals were moving slowly in the cold. A dragonfly nymph clung to the stem of a splatterdock leaf. A water strider made six dents on the surface with its black feet as it walked. Craig thought about the water strider: he might make big feet for himself and his friends so they could walk across the water to Batta—but he did not get very far with the idea. He was diverted by memories of more successful devices he had borrowed from the animals of the swamp and woods.

For instance, the day the marsh buggy was on its maiden voyage. The craft was steady on the water as he and Phil and Steve and Johnny nailed the last plank down and stepped aboard. The motor started, the paddle wheel turned, and they were off with cheers down the channel among the reeds. Too late, they realized they had no way to steer. They were headed for the reeds. Steve jumped to turn off the motor but he was not fast enough. They struck hard, and Craig, standing precariously on the edge, was plunged into the water. He sat up to his chin in mud and black marsh water.

An argument had started aboard the craft. Johnny wanted to lie on his belly and steer with his hands, but Steve thought the best solution was a car steering wheel with ropes attached to two boards nailed beneath so they would turn. Craig had said nothing. He was

watching a water boatman steer itself un-
erringly around the cattail stalks. He leaned
closer to it. Two large feet shaped like paddles
maneuvered the insect. On each foot was a
fringe of hairs that bent to give the creature
more control. "Hey!" he called. "I got it." He
came to his feet dripping black water. "We
need two old canoe paddles. We put one on
each side of the buggy and steer with them."

Steve had nodded. Johnny had said, "That's
it!" and Phil had added, "Where'll we get 'em?"

Johnny suggested that the sporting goods
store might have some secondhand ones they'd
be glad to sell cheap, which they did. In fact,
Mr. Aronozo took only a dollar for them to
hurry the boys out of the store before they
blocked the entrance admiring the guns. Craig,
still impressed by the hairs on the feet of the
boatmen, insisted that they tack fringed inner
tubing on the paddle edges. Johnny had said,
"Okay, you do it." So he did, and fastened the
paddles to the barge with rainspout hoops.
That was two years ago. The beginning of
project Batta.

Craig came out of his thoughts and again
listened for his friends. As he stood up, he
looked back at the buggy and remembered
the day they had finally set sail successfully
through the vast marsh. The motor had purred,

the wheel turned, and the swamp buggy had inched forward on a perfect course. He and his friends had sung songs as they moved down the channel between the reeds. Occasionally they stopped to hack down cattails and make a wider passageway. They puttered on.

The channel wound in and out for a hundred yards among all types of swamp life. Frogs rested on broken reeds, turtles basked in the sun. Occasionally the paddle wheel struck the bulrushes and red-winged blackbirds flew up, protesting the intrusion. There were snakes, muskrats, snails, and dragonflies. As they explored, they talked about the fact that the town board had once wanted to drain this beautiful marsh. If the subject ever came up again, Johnny had said, he would tell his father he would tie himself to the reeds and just stay there.

They turned a bend and came into a huge body of black water, too deep for reeds, too meandering to be a lake—the slow stream. They could see across it to the north shore where the hemlocks darkened the ridge. Ducks floated on the water, a marsh wren sang its pensive song. Craig whispered that they could not see a house or a chimney, for the town was hidden beyond the edge of tall hickories, maples, snakeroots, and rushes.

Then he saw the island! Johnny saw it at the same time. Phil and Steve turned at their shouts. The island was small and green. Its northern end was rocks and boulders; they could see meadow and woods, gold and dappled with sunlight. Craig noticed that the shoreline was covered with moss.

They steered toward it, knowing before they got there that they had found a haven, a place to be alone, a secret island, hidden in the middle of a busy town.

The swamp buggy touched the island and Craig turned off the motor. Softly, he stepped ashore. A flock of ducks winged up, circled the island, then disappeared into the marsh. A raccoon, sunning itself on a sugar maple limb, got up and walked headfirst down the tree. He disappeared along his private trail. The boys tied the buggy to a willow and crept up the embankment. Craig found a sparrow's nest in a hawthorn bush. Four fat babies lifted their heads to be fed as he jiggled their nest branch. Johnny laughed. "Do they think that shaking's their mother?" Craig nodded, and crept on. A mink ran across an opening in front of them. It slipped into the water without a splash.

The island, Steve figured, was about an acre. Most of it was low and flat except for the boulders they had seen from the slow stream. These were high. They jutted above the willows and were surrounded with big hemlocks and saplings, wild grapes and blueberries. The boys climbed the rocks and sat down. "This is heaven," Johnny said. "A boy's acre to try it alone. No piano lessons, no organized activities . . . nothing . . . but us."

"Boy's acre to try it alone," repeated Phil. "Not bad. B–A–T–T–I–A—Battia. Let's name the island Battia."

"Or Batta," said Steve. "That's easier to say."

They spent the rest of the afternoon exploring and rolling in the sun. Reeds jangled, leaves made shadows, ducks and geese cried out, and the herons stalked fish on their long legs.

Before they started back Steve asked to circle the rock once more. On the far side the boulder hung over the ground, making a dry shelter. He called the others. When they found him, he was kneeling in soft earth, digging. "Something's down here," he said. "Gimme a hand."

Suddenly a barrel of dirt shifted under Steve's knees and slid into a deep hole. Craig crept forward on his stomach and peered into the earth. A stone room lay below him. He eased himself down and found six log steps. They spiraled into the room. He lit a match. The light fell on an arched cavern, its floor covered with ages of fine dust. "Gee!" Johnny had followed Craig. "What is it?" Steve and Phil were close behind.

"We've got a secret, a big, quiet secret. Batta, the underground retreat!" Phil said.

"It looks like a Revolutionary War ammunition shelter," observed Steve.

Johnny walked into the room. "I see beds here and a kitchen there. Running water, lights. Wow, we'll never have to go home."

"And it's a good place for the transceiver Uncle Harry gave me," Steve added. He was feeling the dryness of the rocks.

"Yeah, we can listen to music while we fall asleep," said Johnny.

Craig sighed at the memory of that wonderful day two years ago. Now, he thought, we're getting that same wonderful island ready for police inspection. Nuts.

He listened with annoyance for his friends. They were already fifteen minutes late. A water nymph caught his eye. The lower lip of the insect sat far out. The nymph was moving the lip up and under a snail. When the snail rested on it, the insect opened its mouth, and the entire lower lip enclosed the food like a box trap. Pretty tricky, Craig mused, and wondered where such a device could be used in Batta.

Then the willow branches snapped. He jumped at the sound. Steve was saying hello. He had pliers in his hand and Johnny had a shovel and some gunny sacks. They quickly got on the buggy and started the motor. It sputtered and hummed. Slowly it edged down the darkening reed canal. Craig felt the fright and worry of the afternoon disappear as the buggy toiled along. Ducks gabbled in the shadows, a muskrat swam ahead. Craig turned on his flash to light their route through the dark labyrinths of cattails. Johnny hummed a soft tune through his teeth and braces. Then he stopped. "Did I tell you what I discovered at the dentist's yesterday?" he said.

"What?"

"Well, Doctor North was putting a new brace on me when it touched my back filling and I heard 'Yeah, yeah, yeah; stomp stomp.' I looked at the doctor. He wasn't singing so I said with my mouth full, ' 'old it!' He did and I heard the rest of the song. I told him, and *was* he amazed! He said he'd read about this at dental school. Certain kinds of fillings act like crystal sets. But he had never had a patient that got tuned in. He wanted to hear too, but of course he couldn't."

Craig looked back at Johnny. He had never heard such a wonderful story. "Wouldn't you know it," he said. "You get tuned in to the radio waves! Wow!"

"Lucky guy," Steve said, laughing with pleasure. "You can listen to the radio while you're doing your homework. What stations do you get?"

"I dunno, fourteen-fifty, I think." Johnny closed his mouth smugly and grinned at his friends.

"Can you get it now?" asked Craig.

"No, it only happens when something metal touches the filling—like the brace. It's too solid now."

"Shucks," said Craig and tried to peer into Johnny's mouth. "You oughta get him to wire you up for WZIK. Then you could listen to the ball games."

They putted into the slow stream, and Craig lowered the light, for they could see now they were on open water.

Johnny pulled hard on his paddle. "What didja think of Officer Ricardo?" he asked.

Steve said he thought he was pretty nice, and if they made a good show he would probably let them put the rocket off. Craig admitted he liked him but said he was worried about Mr. Brundage. "He's pretty high principled," he said. "In fact, *very* high principled!"

The swamp buggy softly bumped the

wooden wharf on the island. Johnny began to whistle as if the water-locked acre of land had already made him peaceful, but Craig could not forget the huge policeman and all the laws and regulations he stood for. It seemed that there was so much that had to be learned the hard way.

4 BOOSTER NUMBER ONE

Craig's fingers fumbled as he tied the swamp buggy. He mumbled a few reassuring words to himself and slowly walked down the cobblestone path to the launch pit. He stumbled, looked down at the round stones he and his friends had carefully dug into the ground, and was proud to notice how neat they were after two freezing and heaving winters. A dandelion, its head half-blown, was wedged between two stones. He pulled it up and wound through the willow grove to the alders that grew at the edge of the meadow.

The fire control bunker, the observation bunker, and the launching pit sat in the meadow. They were earth-colored and dark against the yellow-green of the grasses, for each was made of mud-filled gunny sacks, dried in the sun and stacked like adobe blocks. Steve, who had run ahead, was at the fire control bunker. Johnny was at the pit, legs apart, hands on his head, thinking. Craig paused again, glanced down the path that led into the hemlock grove, and he felt secretive about the rendezvous at its end—Batta.

"Hurry up, Craig!" Johnny called. Craig doubled his pace to the launch pit and jumped in. The rocket stood before him. Almost three feet tall, it rose out of a ring of six first-stage rockets to stand like a spear in the dusk. The payload and nose cone were not on the booster; they lay in the equipment box. But even without these the rocket looked regal to Craig.

"I should think Officer Ricardo would okay that," he said to Johnny. "And this, too," he added as he kicked the wall of mud bags.

Johnny circled, examining them critically, to see if they would pass inspection. "I *know* they're strong," he said. "Nearly busted my back on 'em." He turned to Craig. "But what about the bottom of the pit? We don't have mud bags on the floor."

"Heck," said Craig, "we spent a whole day pouring water on it and tamping it with those logs. We've always thought it was okay. We can't worry about the floor now. Let's cover the door to Batta." He pushed back the rocket cover, a large corrugated iron pipe cut in half and welded to four legs on old wagon wheels by their friend Joe, a welder.

They squatted down to examine the small wooden door that opened onto the tunnel leading into their underground retreat.

"We don't have time to dry out gunny sacks of mud," said Johnny. "Maybe we'd just better hang them over the door."

Steve had come from the fire control bunker and was standing on the rim, arms folded, listening. "No," he said. "Officer Ricardo might look behind them. We've gotta fill the bags with dirt and stack them as best we can."

"You're right," said Johnny and leaped out of the pit, dragging the gunny sacks. He picked up the shovel and started across the meadow toward the beach and the clay deposits.

Steve opened the door to Batta and crawled down the passageway. In a few minutes he was back with a board. "I'm gonna build a shelf for the launch panel," he announced, as he balanced it on his head and walked toward the fire control bunker. He stopped halfway and swung around. "By the way!" he called, "as of this minute the fire control bunker is officially the Batta Command Center."

Craig nodded, and stared into the equipment box with a vague plan in his head.

"Hey! Help!" It was Johnny. "I can't lift the durn bag."

Craig laughed and ran to him. He skidded down the beach and grabbed a side of the filled sack. He heaved. They both heaved, then sat down. "This isn't gonna work," Craig said. "I'd forgotten how heavy the earth is, and the rollers we used on the other bags are now pilings in the wharf."

"Think!" cried Johnny. "It's almost dark. Durn it, Craig, you're the guy who steals ideas from the animals. What does a box turtle or a rabbit do when it wants to hide?"

"They're disguised. Also, they sit still."

"Well, let's disguise the door then," said Johnny.

"How?"

"I don't know. Tack the countdown data sheets on it, or something."

Craig lifted his head slowly. "And below the

sheets," he said, "we nail tubes and dials and condensers from the equipment box to make a fake instrument panel."

"Go! It's go!" Johnny shouted and was up the beach and away before Craig could get to his feet.

Craig hummed to himself as he and Johnny set happily to work, nailing a strange assemblage of equipment to the door.

"Hey!" Steve called suddenly. "I can't see. Somebody put on the lights. I can't leave this shelf or it'll fall."

Craig and Johnny stopped work and crossed the meadow to the thicket of maples. As they came to the grove of hemlocks, Craig heard an animal scurry over the huge boulders on their right. "The 'coon's up," he said and put his hand on the doorknob of a cabin marked "Power House." The knob was an old coil loop antenna that Mr. Pappo had given them. Craig turned it and it clicked out of the notch in a small condenser below it. The door opened.

They went in the cabin, made from logs notched at the ends for stability. Each fitted into the other, and they were chinked with the red-gray clay from the beach.

Johnny lit a candle while Craig primed a gasoline camp stove. When it flamed up he put on a strange-looking teakettle and waited for the sound of boiling water. At the hiss he pressed a plug and cord into a fitting on the kettle. Gradually two 40-watt bulbs at the end of a long cord began to glow, then rose to full brightness. Johnny blew out the candle and shouldered the cord and bulbs. He chuckled.

"Remember when Mr. Brian helped us make this thing?"

"Yeah." Craig pretended to recite a science lesson. "If the contact point of two unlike metals is heated one can turn steam into electricity. That was the day!"

They walked back to the launching pit, reeling out the cord carefully. As Craig studied the light he remembered those days after school with Mr. Brian when they built the power system. "The Science Academy" they had dubbed themselves while they made the thermoelectric teakettle. Using a blowtorch, they had removed the original bottom of the kettle, had soldered on the two unlike metals. Then they had wired it. When it was done Mr. Pappo came to see it. He took notes in case one of his companies would be interested in manufacturing something like it for ski shacks and camping. He didn't ask the boys what they planned to do with it, so they took it to Batta, added enough wire to get the lights around most of the island, and built a cabin for it.

But Mr. Pappo warned them that such a device should be used near a fire extinguisher, and Mr. Brian had suggested making one. Phil offered a discarded extinguisher from his home. The class rebuilt and refueled it. Several days later, when the class was on another project, Phil had brought it to Batta.

Johnny nudged Craig to stop dreaming and help. He hung one light over the rim of the launching pit and took the other one to Steve. Then Craig and Johnny went back to their construction of a bogus instrument panel to cover the tunnel entrance. Craig picked up a large dial, told Johnny it was a receiver, and screwed it onto the door.

"I'm jealous," said Johnny. He drove three nails into the door and pressed a big radio tube between them. "Ha!" he said with satisfaction.

Craig looked at it enviously, and he took out some wire for a new creation. Presently Steve joined them. "The Batta Command Center is all set!" he announced. "I'm using the old battery we got from the Telephone Surplus Department for power. I guess it's strong enough."

"What's the matter with Mom's car battery?" Craig asked as he crisscrossed some wire from his dial to Johnny's tube.

"It's still attached to the transceiver. Too

much trouble to change." Steve leaned over Johnny's shoulder. He laughed at the sight before him. "What are you gonna say it does?" he asked with pleasure. "Looks spectacular."

"Yeah, what'll we say this thing does?" Johnny asked Craig.

"Tell 'im the truth," Craig promptly replied. "Tell him it's a fake panel to pretend on. Everybody thinks we're pretending anyway." He stood beside Johnny to observe the work.

"Well, it sure doesn't look like a door anymore," said Steve.

"You can say that again, but what does it look like?"

"A panel to control the weege on the strandfast," Craig answered. "It muckles the third bango and hikes the throughpower."

"It also yawls the pocket trivel," said Johnny.

"And reeds the apple picker," added Steve.

"But mainly," roared Johnny, "it buttons down the curiosity!"

They laughed and threw their arms around each other. Then they put away their tools, pulled the cover over the rocket, and went to the dock. It was almost ten o'clock; the night was moonless and dark.

Steve started the motor, and Craig, still thinking of nonsense sentences, unhitched the line. He shoved Johnny firmly onto the swamp buggy and sat down beside him. "Come on, Einstein, give me some room."

"Silence!" shouted Steve. His voice was ominously serious. "We must agree on one other thing. Do we tell Officer Ricardo all the secrets about the rocket?"

"No," said Craig. "Enough's enough."

"No!" echoed Johnny.

"All right then, but we gotta show him something. Is it all right with you guys if I get out the diagram showing how we built the booster?"

"Sure," Johnny said, "all that stuff's impressive."

Craig hunched over his knees as he leveled the guiding flashlight into the reeds. He thought with pride of the diagrams and maps, the graphs and calculations. He could see the admiration on everyone's face, especially Mr. Brundage's, and he heard a barrage of adult voices saying, "Let them put it off. It's wonderful!"

He was grinning to himself when the craft drifted into a flock of sleeping ducks, heads under their wings, rafted on the water like loaves of bread. They thrust up their necks at the sound of the swamp buggy, then passed worried gabbles among themselves. Craig swung his light around the flock. They jumped quickly onto their wings and feet and skimmed over the water. A single duck, rafted beyond the others, was still sleeping. Craig threw the light on him, and his head went up. Wide-eyed with sudden fear, the bird did not wing off, but sat still. Craig was perplexed. He decided that there sat a duck who would soon be prey to some dark predator. It did not heed the signals of its flock. And that's bad, he said to himself.

"For gosh sakes!" Steve suddenly shouted. "Turn that light on the reeds or we'll be spending the night with the durn ducks and herons!"

Craig obeyed with a laugh. He was so proud of their rocket, so absolutely sure that anyone who saw it would approve, that nothing could upset him.

In the darkness Johnny's hand gripped his shoulder. Craig could feel Johnny's pride and excitement, too. He shone the beam into the channel and whistled softly.

5 THE INSPECTION

Officer Ricardo was prompt. At eleven o'clock the next day Steve leaned out the second-story window of Craig's house and announced, "One white police car. Red light, green, and going."

"Gee!" Craig jumped off his bed where he had been stretched out, waiting tensely. His stomach whirled and turned as he also leaned out the window next to Steve and saw the big officer open his patrol car door and unfold. His chest came above the roof of the car.

"We'll be right down," Steve called.

He cleared his throat and walked out of the room. Craig followed, his confidence of the night before somewhat pierced.

Officer Ricardo was waiting for them at the bottom of the path. "I guess we'd better leave the squad car and walk," he said. "It's out of the way here."

Johnny was sitting on the side of the road when they came down the hill. Craig was relieved to see him rise confidently and shake the officer's hand with a firm "Hello." Johnny, he could see, felt fine. Craig decided he felt better, too.

"This way, sir," Johnny said and pointed to the hidden trail. "We have to go by boat."

"Oh," said the officer. "What've you got, a rowboat?" No one knew how to answer him, so they simply stepped up their pace to the wharf, uncovered the swamp buggy, and turned, grinning, for his response.

"You made it?" he asked.

"Yes, sir," said Steve proudly. "Just hop aboard." He held out his hand for the big man.

Officer Ricardo sat squarely in the center of the raft and brought his knees up to his chin.

Craig sensed he was uneasy so he did not jump onto the craft in his usual way, but eased to the rear and took a paddle. Johnny started the motor. Steve unhitched the line.

Craig saw Officer Ricardo look suspiciously at the big wheel as it slowly turned and dug into the water. "This is a fine boat," he said. "Clever." But his knuckles were white as they clenched his knees. Craig racked his mind for a way to relax him. From the cove ahead, he heard the gabbling of the ducks.

"Hey," Craig cried, "be quiet along here. You'll see the finest assortment of ducks in the county." He reached into his pocket and brought out some birdseed, waited until they turned the corner in view of the birds, and tossed it.

There was a flash of color as some fifty to sixty ducks pivoted and swam toward the flying seeds. "Canvas ducks, mallards, blacks, two mergansers, and a blue-winged teal," Craig said. "Lots of them gather here on their migration. No one but us bothers them. And we're their friends."

Craig threw another handful of seed. The buggy tilted slightly and Officer Ricardo grabbed the floor. His frightened movement was sensed by the ducks. They turned and winged over the water into the splatterdock plants. Steve leaned to the left to counteract the tilt, and the craft settled back.

"Sorry," said Craig, "but don't be nervous. She's really impossible to upset."

"Good drums," said Johnny, kicking one.

The swamp buggy edged out into the slow stream that gleamed like a sheet of black metal.

"Well!" Officer Ricardo murmured. "I didn't know all this was here. It's beautiful. Just beautiful!" The buggy purred along evenly and Craig felt the officer relax.

Then the island came into view. "Not bad," the officer said, "you've got something here. A quiet island in the middle of a driving busy town. Nice." He let go of his knees and took a long deep breath of air.

They eased gently up to the wharf and Johnny leaped off. He offered the officer his hand, but the man refused and jumped nimbly to the dock.

"Hmmm," he said, looking at the wharf and pilings. "Very good!" He tested one of the piles. It did not budge.

Steve seemed glad for this first impression. He brightened up as he took over. "Come this way," he said and led the group down the cobblestone trail.

Craig held up the rear, peering around Johnny's shoulder now and then to see what the policeman was doing. He saw his head move from side to side as he crossed the meadow, noting the observation bunker, the command center, and finally the launching pit.

"Well," he said as he came up to the rim of the pit, "what do we have here? A rocket?"

"Yes, sir," said Steve with some surprise in his voice. "Isn't that what you were expecting?"

"Not exactly," the officer said and stepped into the pit. Craig and Johnny moved quickly to pull back the cover so he would not strike his head. Then they watched him. Officer Ricardo turned around many times. He saw the countdown sheet and began to read aloud, "T-minus twelve. Pack flameproof recovery wadding into the body tube." He looked up. He looked directly at Craig, then his glance passed on to Johnny, then Steve.

"You all aren't kidding, are you?" he said. There was some anger in his voice.

"Well, no," said Johnny. "We never said we were."

Officer Ricardo spun around slowly. He stopped and stared. "You should've told me," he said. "This thing's a rocket!"

"Yes," said Steve. He shifted his feet. "Perhaps we should explain." He jumped into the pit beside the policeman and pointed to the booster. "This is a three-stage booster rocket. Stage one surrounds it in this circle of tubes. Two and three are in the tall rocket. The payload isn't here. We keep it separately. There are twenty-four engines in this particular rocket, and they ought to get the rocket up two thousand, if not three thousand, feet."

"I see," the officer said.

"The rocket is launched from a command station," Steve went on as he walked toward the bunker. Craig nudged Johnny, for Officer Ricardo was staring at the disguised door and scratching his head. Steve called, "Here we have an ignition control panel that sets the rocket off from a safe distance, that is, from behind this wall of mud bags." He slapped them. Officer Ricardo slapped them, too, then turned his attention to the slender ignition control with its switches and needles.

"These wires," said Steve pointing, "have microclips on the ends. They are attached to the engines, and when the current goes through them, they heat up, and zowie! Off goes the rocket! It's that simple."

"I see," said Officer Ricardo. Steve grinned. The officer leaned over the ignition panel. "Where did you get this?"

"We made it," broke in Johnny. "We all

saved dimes and nickels from our lunch money and bought the kit—it only cost about four dollars."

"Oh."

"That's about all there is to it," concluded Steve. The officer thumped the bags once more, looked closely at them, and pondered. Presently he returned to the launch pit and sat down on the rim, his feet inside.

"Well, now," he said seriously. Craig was glad to hear firmness in his voice, for it no longer implied that he thought they were playing with firecrackers or CO_2 cartridges. "Suppose the thing goes crooked and shoots off toward Blue Springs?" he said to Steve.

"We have a relay radio device," Steve said. "It'll blow 'er up over the swamp if anything goes wrong."

"I see." Officer Ricardo stiffened and stared at Steve. "Well, then," he continued, "where will the rocket come down—on the school?— the shopping center?"

Steve opened the equipment box and took out the drawings and diagrams. "It comes down here," he said, and traced with his finger a triangulation of the flight on the map.

The officer studied them. "May I have these?" he asked. "I'd like to show them to the chief and Mr. Brundage." Craig pulled closer into the circle. It sounded as if the officer were coming over to their side.

Steve showed him some more diagrams. Between each lesson Officer Ricardo dropped the papers onto his knees and stared at the dials on the door to Batta. Then he resumed his concentration.

"Gosh, Steve," he finally said, "I'm lost. I'm not the person to decide this. It's too complicated."

"You don't have to understand it," insisted Steve. "You can see it's safe. Even if it blew up on the launch pad, we'd all be behind mud barriers; and that's about the worst that could happen way out here."

"I dunno, I dunno." The officer shook his head.

"Aw, shucks," said Johnny. "It's okay, Officer Ricardo, all you have to do is tell the chief that. We can vouch for it."

The officer smiled at Johnny. "Well, I'll tell you what I'll do. I'll make a report and take this into the chief and Mr. Brundage. They just might agree since it's way out here." He took out his notebook. "Now, let's go through this again. How tall is the rocket?"

Steve spoke more slowly this time. Craig listened and grinned at Johnny from time to time as his hopes climbed.

At last Mr. Ricardo stuck his pencil in his jacket. "Is there anything else I should see," he said, "before I decide to stretch out in the meadow for a week?" He yawned.

"Would you like to see the powerhouse?" asked Johnny.

"Sure." He got up. "I suppose you're going to tell me now that you generate electricity."

"Well, yes," said Johnny. He brushed off his trousers and beckoned to the officer.

Mr. Ricardo hesitated as he examined the cabin, but this time he did not even ask whether they had made it. Instead, he thumped the logs critically and went inside. Johnny explained the thermoelectric teakettle that converted steam into electricity. The officer listened quietly. Finally he mumbled, "I feel very old."

Half an hour later Craig helped Officer Ricardo onto the swamp buggy, and this time the big man sat down on the craft with confidence. They sailed gently back.

Craig was tired when they reached the police car, but nevertheless he was eager for some reassurance. "Can we?" he asked brightly.

The officer looked at him, reached in his car, and switched on his two-way radio. "Officer Ricardo to chief. Ricardo to chief. Over."

"Come in, Mission Firecracker. Well, what's with the Roman candle department? Over."

"I don't understand anything," Officer Ricardo blared, "but we have an astonishment on our hands. Suggest Brundage form the committee. Over."

"Yeah? What've they done? Over."

"Get me a man with a Ph.D. in electronics and send him out here. There's an instrument panel that's so complicated I can't even ask a leading question about it. Over."

Craig felt his stomach drop.

"Come on in, Ricardo. Over and out."

Officer Ricardo switched off his mike. He leaned out the door. "I'll look into it further," he said. "And I'll call you soon." He winked at them. The tires spun on the gravel in the lane as the police car departed.

"Well," said Johnny, "I might as well go home and practice the piano, rake the yard, and join the drama club." He turned and walked away.

Craig watched him go. "He's upset. He's really upset. I can always tell. He's gonna practice!"

"Well, I'm not discouraged yet," said Steve. "He did say he'd call us soon. And that means 'go' to me."

Craig looked at him sharply and saw that he

was not as confident as his words sounded. Craig sighed and turned away. "So long," he said to Steve. "See ya." He walked up the steps and paused at the door. Steve's voice followed him.

"You and your animal inventions!" Steve said. "Our famous panel flubbed the whole thing."

Craig shrugged his shoulders and went through the door.

6 THE LARGE MEN

Phil came to school on Monday with a heavy heart. He decided to avoid his friends. He had no desire to talk about the awful week end and the consequences of his telling his father they were about to launch a rocket. As he came around the corner of the building, however, he ran into Craig, whose mother was letting him off at the front door. Craig ducked him, ran up the steps, and pushed through the swinging door.

Phil watched him go, and although it hurt, he guessed he deserved it. Phil was a year older than Craig and Johnny, and he had grown rapidly the past winter. He was a head taller than Johnny and he had discovered that this added height was excellent for expressing his state of mind. He could roll his shoulders over to make himself smaller when he felt hurt or angry, or he could lift them and swing them wide when he felt good. At this moment his shoulders curled forward.

At three o'clock as he was leaving his locker he heard his name called. He turned and saw Craig. Phil wondered what he should say, but he didn't have a chance to think it out.

"Listen, Phil," Craig said, "you better beat it straight home today. Officer Ricardo's coming to see your father. He inspected the rocket, you know."

"Whatdidhesay?" Phil was hungry for his friends and for news of their project.

"Well, sort of 'yes' and sort of 'no.' Anyway, he called Mom this morning to ask her how she felt about it all. Said he was gonna see your dad this afternoon." Craig paused. "Sorry I ducked you this morning. But it's just so durn embarrassing to be brought to school by Mom. I was trying to make it to the bushes so no one could see me when you came along." He grinned sheepishly.

"I understand," Phil mumbled. "We all got our problems." He straightened up and slapped Craig's shoulder. "Thanks for the headlines about Dad. See ya." And he ran to catch the bus.

As Phil hurried toward his house from the bus stop he saw Officer Ricardo's car parked outside. The officer was standing on the lawn under the gold hickory tree. Stippled light fell on his shoulders. He was staring at the big brick and clapboard house set against the far side of the northern ridge that cradled the marsh.

"You know," Officer Ricardo said as Phil approached him, "coming to your house about a rocket seems a little silly at this point." He looked up at the wide lawn and the trimmed bushes. "When I was a kid I grew up on the streets of the Bronx. We exploded firecrackers, ran between cars for balls, played jokes on the local merchants, and outran the cops whose duty it was to catch us and bring us to justice —by the ears."

Phil didn't quite understand. "You mean you're here to arrest us?"

"No, not at all, I don't mean that," the officer said. "I mean, so far nobody has done anything, so I don't know why I'm here. I'm acting like a mother, not a cop." He turned as if he thought he would go back to his car.

"Please, sir," Phil begged when he saw him start away, "talk to Dad. Tell him that the rocket is safe. I sure want the fellows to put it off after the mess I've gotten them into."

Officer Ricardo took off his cap and ran his fingers through his hair. He scratched the side of his round nose and rubbed his jaw. "All right. I'm this far. I guess I'll at least talk to your father."

Phil opened the front door. "Dad!" he called toward the library. "Police Officer Ricardo is here."

Mr. Brundage was tall, big-boned, and, at this moment, expressionless. As he came forward he seemed to Phil to be wading an ocean of reluctance.

"Good day," he said, looking the officer over. "I like a big man," he commented as they shook hands.

Phil was surprised to notice that his father's eyes were level with the policeman's. It gave Phil a strange feeling to see his father in scale with another man. Even his father's gestures, which always seemed forceful and big, were modest enough as Officer Ricardo swung off his cap and barn-doored into the living room. Phil watched him sit down in one of the ample chairs.

The officer squared himself in the chair, leaned over to examine its structure, and said, "Comfortable. I'm glad to see someone else knows how to buy chairs."

Mr. Brundage's face lighted in appreciation of their common problem. Phil thought perhaps they might get along. He sat on the stairs.

"What I can't understand," Mr. Brundage began to a boom, "is how these boys got a rocket assembled and ready to fire without anyone knowing about it."

"Well"—Officer Ricardo scratched his head—"the funny thing about it is that almost the whole town is involved one way or another. I don't think any of the people who helped knew they were helping, but there were teachers, merchants, laborers."

"Teachers, merchants, laborers?" echoed Mr. Brundage. "How did they get into it? Why wasn't I called? After all, my own son was involved." He stood up and began to pace back and forth. "Rockets are dangerous. States are trying to outlaw them." His feet pounded an emphasis to his words. "I sat on a committee of statesmen and scientists in Albany three years ago. And they were all crying to the pulpit and the press to help end this. I gave several sermons on the dangers of dry fuels and kids.

"And now—here is my own son, and a bunch of his uninformed friends, making a rocket right here amongst us. And behind my back. Officer, how could such a thing happen in this community?"

Officer Ricardo, Phil observed, was studying the path that his father was carving in the rug. "Us big men," the officer said calmly, "sure can be hard on the carpets."

Mr. Brundage paid no attention. He went on, in a voice that got louder and louder. "In this town where kids have everything—friends, things to do, excursions, gadgets, everything— they go out and make an instrument of destruction. Why? Tell me, why?"

"Well, I will," the officer finally shouted back. He got to his feet and looked the minister in the eyes. "If I may! They wanted to do something on their own—without so durn much supervision. That's why!"

He snapped his arms over his chest. Phil could see that the doubts Officer Ricardo had had when they spoke on the lawn had been replaced by a definite stand on the matter. He was with them.

Mr. Brundage dropped his head. "I know," he said, "I know. I guess it's no worse than when we were kids setting off a batch of Roman candles behind the barn." He plunged into a chair. "Let's have the facts, Officer. What did you see?"

"A three-stage booster rocket," Officer Ricardo said, reading his notes, "an ignition control panel, a nose cone, a thermoelectric teakettle, and a vast instrument panel. Vast. And, oh," with a deadpan face, "the balsa nose cones that you helped to carve."

Phil's father pulled forward in the chair. "I helped to carve nose cones? Never in your life." He leaned back.

"That's what the boys said."

"Phil!" boomed Mr. Brundage. "Come here!"

Phil rose stiff-kneed from his listening post on the stairs. He ran his fingers through his tight brown curls and flared his nostrils to give his face a harder look. His shoulders rounded unconsciously as he came down the steps and walked up to his father.

"Officer Ricardo tells me I carved cones for this rocket," his father said sternly.

"Yes. You did."

"When, for heaven's sake?"

"Last Christmas vacation. You were teaching me how to use a knife and to whittle away from my chest. We were copying nose cones out of that manual. Remember?"

"Yes . . . I do . . . but nose cones for a rocket? That was only a joke, a little example to try the blade on. It wasn't anything serious." Mr. Brundage laughed unconvincingly.

"*I* took it seriously," said Phil. He was beginning to feel anxious again as he faced his father.

"Is this how the whole thing got built? I mean, didn't anyone know what you all were putting them up to?"

"We weren't putting anyone up to anything. I asked you if we could carve cones for a rocket and you said 'sure, that would be very constructive.' In fact, you said we'd carve the best nose cones in the nation!"

"Hmmm, sounds like me. When I don't think about what I'm doing I say things I don't mean."

"No, you don't," Phil insisted. He had never before heard his father say such a thing. "I asked you to teach me how to use a knife on balsa nose cones. And you did. And I used them."

"Yes." The minister pondered. "Nevertheless, it's another matter now. Twenty-four engines! And what about all those instruments on the panel? What do they do?"

Phil rubbed the side of his leg and wondered what instrument panel. He could only guess that Officer Ricardo had been impressed by the fire control panel. "Well, that's what launches it and makes it safe."

Phil could see that whatever he had said had perplexed the officer. His eyes were widening and his mouth was pursing into a whistle. "All I can say," Officer Ricardo announced, "is that that rocket must be a humdinger to need all that control."

Phil could feel his father tense at those words. The muscles along his jawbone rippled and his lips tightened, a family forecast of trouble.

"Phil!" his father said, "do you know about the tensile strength of the metals you're dealing with? What do you do if it goes off course and heads toward homes?"

His face was stern. "Can you trace it? Can you say the metal will not explode?"

Phil ran his hands through his curls and shifted his weight from his left foot to his right. "Well . . . it's not met—"

"Who's tested it?"

"Well, us," Phil said tentatively.

His father glared in astonishment.

"No one," Phil whispered.

"No one!" his father boomed. "And do you think you can set this off?"

Phil began to stutter. This made him angry,

for it always gave the advantage to his opponent in an argument.

"And you, too, Officer Ricardo," said Mr. Brundage, turning to face the officer. The minister was angry now.

"Now, just a minute, Mr. Brundage," the policeman shouted as he rose from the big chair. "I've seen this thing. It's an accomplishment!"

"And you think you are able to judge metals and heats and velocities, Mr. Ricardo?"

"I didn't say that!" yelled the officer. "I just said you ought to see it, too. You'd be proud! And I've just come to say," his voice continued to mount, "that I think your suggestion of a committee of parents is good, and that you ought to get them together, because," he rose on his toes so that he was a little taller than Phil's father, "because I don't understand one durn thing they're doing."

Mr. Brundage stared at him. Phil could see that Officer Ricardo had been heard. His father turned his back and paced again. "I'm in a lousy position," he said quietly. "You understand, don't you, Mr. Ricardo?"

"Yes," he answered. "I really do. When can you get the committee together?"

"I'll call them tonight."

Phil stepped back as the two men strode toward the door.

"Of course," said his father, "these members of the committee are busy. They are busy men. It may take some time before we can all arrange our schedules. But we will. Be assured."

Officer Ricardo gestured with both palms open. "It's your kid," he said. "Let me know when you get the committee together." He pulled open the door. Then he swung his big chin over his shoulder. "Sir, lemme tell you something. Committees and democracies are great in Albany and Washington, but they don't have anxious kids waiting for decisions, and you know how slow committees in this town can be."

"I am fully aware."

Officer Ricardo put on his cap. Phil's father walked through the doorway with him. He called to a small brown dog straining and barking at the end of a rope, "Chess, be quiet!" Mr. Brundage shook the officer's hand, and Phil heard him say, "I'll call you as soon as the committee is able to meet. And thanks for your concern."

His father went back to his library. Phil sat down on the steps and said, "Phew!"

7 FOGGED IN

A week passed. It was October first. The sugar maples were scarlet to their green-black trunks. The hickory leaves had fallen to the ground. The houses of Blue Springs emerged from the leafy camouflage of summer to show their sidings, bright and checkered with aluminum sashes.

Each day of the week Craig had waited for Phil at the swinging doors of the school. Craig did not have to ask whether Mr. Brundage had called the committee together. He could tell by the way Phil moved as he came up the walk. Monday he shrugged. Tuesday he turned the palms of his hands outward. Wednesday he walked up the steps with his head down. Thursday he revived and flung back his arms humorously. Friday he went in the janitor's door.

By Saturday Craig was confused and let-down. He leaned on his window sill and felt coldness in the blowing wind. Winter was coming. The rocket was doomed to sit on its launching pad forever. Then he thought gratefully of the meeting he would have with Steve, Phil, and Johnny at three. They were going to go to Batta to sit. Meanwhile he had a football game to play. He got up and snatched his uniform.

As he walked out the door, his mother looked up from her account book, saw his helmet, and called, "Be sure to win!"

"Yeah," he said, a little frightened because he knew his team probably would not and he hated to fail his mother. "I'll try."

Craig was tense all through the game. Parents were on the sidelines cheering, children were shouting, and upper classmen were telling them to "Go! Go!" When the game was finally lost, Craig hurried away, for he suddenly knew he hated these games. He was disappointed when they lost, sorry for the other team when they won. Yet he had been told over and over again that playing football was good for him. And he guessed it must be.

But he was glad when he got to Rushing Road. Steve and Phil joined him almost immediately.

"Where's Johnny?" Craig asked.

"His father wants to play pitch," said Steve. He dropped his hands to his sides. " 'Sfunny how fathers think that playing pitch is being a good father," the older boy mused. "I wonder if fathers really like it?"

"I dunno," Craig said. "But I know Johnny would really like his dad to see the rocket." They walked to the wharf.

And there was Officer Ricardo sitting on the dock, a fishing rod in his hand.

"Thought you all might be going out in the swamp buggy this afternoon," he said with a pleasant smile. "So I stopped by to hitch a ride and do some fishin'. Any cats or sunnies out there?"

"Plenty," said Craig. "Guess we all might as well fish." He hesitated to ask about the rocket because he did not want to hear the answer. But he had to know. He put it backwards. "They're not going to inspect the rocket today, are they?"

" 'Fraid not, everybody's awful busy." A silence fell. Officer Ricardo tried to fill it. "But something did happen," he said. Craig and Steve looked at him. "I got a scientist, a man named Smith. He's a model rocket expert."

The officer eased himself into the middle of the craft.

"Smith?" Steve sounded excited. "Mr. Casey Smith? Do you know if he has a daughter named Cathy?" Craig saw Steve redden. Officer Ricardo said yes, the man's name was Casey Smith and that he had run a rocket club in Kansas. He didn't know about a daughter.

Steve started the mower engine. "Kansas," he said. "Yes, he does have a daughter. Her name is Cathy—Cathy Smith." He was smiling. "And she's in my class." Something in Steve's voice made Craig look at him again. The swamp buggy started off and he wasn't sure what he saw.

The wheeling craft churned among the reeds. Over the far ridge a wet bank of clouds hung like a curtain. "Looks like rain," Craig observed. "Should make the fishin' good." He pulled on the paddle and thoughtfully watched a green heron spear a frog. It swallowed the amphibian headfirst. A bump marked the frog's trip down the long throat to the stomach.

Nobody talked. The buggy edged out into

the black water. Craig watched a flock of Canada geese drop out of the low cloud. The birds circled the marsh. Their heads tilted sidewise as they surveyed the water and reeds. Satisfied, they skidded onto the lake, not far from the island. They preened, shook their tails, and honked softly to each other, a sound Craig knew to be a signal of satisfaction. He guessed they had found a good stopover on their way south.

The swamp buggy drifted toward them. Suddenly a large drake, neck back, wings beating, shot at them. The hissing noise he made was ominous.

"Let's get out of here," said Officer Ricardo. "Those things can be durn mean." But the boys were not afraid and they steered closer.

Craig reached in his pocket for a few grains of seed. He threw them on the water. A female shot out and was about to snatch the food, when the male charged her. He chased her into the flock.

"Now, then," said Craig, "that oughta be some sort of lesson to us—like 'might is right.'"

"Or, as my father says," cried Phil, " 'he who honks, gets.' "

"I thought ministers didn't approve of things like that," Officer Ricardo said.

"Oh, they don't," answered Phil. "But it happens all the time. What my father says is 'that's how it is, friends. Fight it as long as you can. Then live with it.' That's what he says."

Craig turned the expression over in his mind. "I guess he feels it's time for us to live with a grounded rocket."

"Maybe," said Phil.

"Not me," said Steve.

The geese disappeared behind the island as the swamp buggy pulled up to the wharf. Craig ran into Batta to get fishing rods. He checked the rocket, covered the ignition panel with a sack, and came back. He noticed as they put out into the wide black water of the marsh that the cloud bank had lowered.

Three hours passed. Officer Ricardo caught two bass and one catfish. He was pleased. "I like to eat cats better'n any fish I know," he said. "I lived all my life in the city till I was out of high school. Then my uncle took me on a boat trip down the Mississippi. We caught catfish and lolled around livin' like kings. Those were the happiest days of my life; just driftin' down the Mississippi from town to town, fishin' hole to fishin' hole for seven whole months!" He sighed and jerked up his line. It was empty. He dropped it back.

"Guess that's why I like this place," he went

on. "It reminds me of the muck and mire and the bird-filled edges of that old river. If I were you fellows, I'd say to heck with the rocket and just come out here and sit and grow straight up." Craig listened. The officer talked on about the night when a band of gypsies took all their food—and the day that he swiped it all back. It was an absorbing story.

Suddenly Craig noticed that the cloud had reached the water and the edges of the marsh were enveloped in fog. It was blowing toward them. "Hey," he said. "We'd better get outa here. That's a real fog."

Steve agreed and pulled in his line, Phil hauled up the anchor, and the buggy labored slowly toward the channel and the wharf.

"It's getting dark," said Officer Ricardo. And then the motor coughed and stopped.

"My gosh, we're out of gas!" moaned Phil. "Is there any in the emergency can?" Steve reached over the side and unhooked a plastic bottle. He shook it.

"No," he answered.

"Well," said Craig, "I was sure those geese had a better message for us than 'might makes right.' Everybody on your stomach and paddle like a goose."

The three boys lined the edge of one side of

the craft, balancing the huge officer on the other. They hollered in unison, "Stroke! Stroke!" The craft crept forward.

After a long time Officer Ricardo looked up. "Which way is the road?" The fog had enveloped them now. Steve lifted his head. "I dunno," he said. "I don't even know which way's up. Looks to me like the sky has fallen."

Darkness obscured everything but a circle of black water a foot from Craig's face.

"Hush," he said. "Listen! The geese are behind the island. Paddle toward that sound."

Everyone strained to hear. Faintly to their right they heard a gabble as the geese kept in touch with each other in the fog. They paddled in that direction.

And at last the swamp buggy struck the island.

"Hoo-ray!" Officer Ricardo said. Craig felt his way ashore and tied up the craft. By the slope of the land, and by the size of the hawthorn bush under his hand, he knew they were about ten feet west of the launching pit. He put Officer Ricardo's left foot on the shore, heard him ground his right, and, knowing he was safe, grabbed the fishing rods and led the way. "Come on," he yelled, and groped his way by limb and stone to the pit. Shuffling and sliding, the others joined him. Then they sat down and rested.

"Now whattam I gonna do?" the officer said. "My wife is expecting me for dinner. We're having guests, and I can't even let her know I'm all right. She's a worrier, too."

"Gee," said Steve. "I guess our folks will figure out where we are; but they don't know you're with us, so that won't help you."

"I'd better try to swim."

"You can't," said Steve. "The water's shallow, sticky mud. Besides, you can't see where you're going." He felt for Craig's knee and poked it. "There's only one thing to do. Right, Craig?"

"Right."

"Phil?"

"Uh." His voice was almost inaudible.

"Officer Ricardo," Steve said, to a blur in the fog, "you asked us why we don't loll around and camp out here. We do. We have a secret hideout on the island. We all promised never to show it to anybody—not anybody. But it looks like we'll have to take you there tonight."

"Well." The man hesitated. "I'm sorry, but I'd sure like to get out of this dampness."

"Craig, lead the way. You're the guy who knows the bushes by the fuzz on their leaves."

Craig edged slowly down the path, past the fogged-in power plant and up to the boulder that loomed like a black behemoth in the mist. Steve turned to Officer Ricardo.

"The main reason we're bringing you here," he said, "is because we have a transceiver here in Batta—that's the name of the hideout—and we might be able to reach the police station and tell them you're all right."

"Wonderful!" Officer Ricardo exclaimed in relief. "I'm really quite concerned about my wife. You see, she's had a bad heart for some time now and I try not to worry her."

"Gee, that is bad," Craig said. "But don't get too excited. We may not be able to reach them. Our range isn't very far."

"We could add some more antennas," Steve suggested. "After all, this *is* an emergency."

Craig fumbled in the dark, found the door to Batta, and whispered to the officer, "Not even your wife? Promise?"

"Not even my wife," repeated Mr. Ricardo.

8 BATTA

Everyone waited while Phil groped his way
back to the powerhouse and brought the lights.
Then they went inside.

The light danced warmly on three walls of
logs, chinked like the powerhouse, with clay
from the beach. The fourth wall was the side
of the boulder.

Craig saw Officer Ricardo glance at photographs of Titan III, drawings of the Batta
booster, and the scale drawings of nose cones

on the walls, then look around for something to sit on.

"This is only the chartroom," Craig said. "Batta is this way." Phil carried the light across the narrow room. It illuminated the steep spiral staircase that plunged into the earth. The hand-carved steps gleamed red-brown.

"Did you make these?" Mr. Ricardo asked.

"No," Steve answered. "The staircase was already here. We dug into an old Revolutionary War ammunition shelter one day and moved in. Come this way." Steve followed Phil down the steps.

"What have you got down here?" Officer Ricardo asked. "A bomb? Is that why it's so secret?"

"No," called Steve. "It's just a place. You know . . . a place to go to. There are no ruffly curtains, no *avant-garde* paintings on the wall, no Chippendale furniture. It's just us."

"I see," the officer said, and he did.

Craig suddenly saw Batta in a new light. The warm brown color in the stones of the staircase shone out. He stepped proudly into the long narrow room, arched like an oatmeal box and sparkling with more gadgets than anyone could take in. Officer Ricardo stood at the bottom of the staircase in silent wonder. Craig crossed the room so he could watch his face.

He was pleased to see that it registered the proper awe. "Just Batta," Phil said with restrained pride.

The policeman moved to the nearest wall and studied a drawing signed by Phil of an entire farm in a spaceship. Then he pondered over the balsa wood model of Gemini II hanging from a thread on the ceiling. Walking slowly, he touched the chair cut from the stump of a willow. He saw a telescope lying on it and picked it up. Craig grinned for he had made it out of a tube from a roll of paper toweling and three lenses he had bought at an optical store. The officer peered through it. He put it down and walked toward the flat rock that jutted out of the far end of the room. It was about four feet high. On it lay three matted-down sheepskins and one elk skin. He paused and examined the lights that hung down over each skin. Phil jumped on the rock and flopped down on his belly.

"This is the bunk," he said. "The lights are wired to six-volt dry cells." He flipped a switch and a lamp went on. A shade of aluminum foil spotted the bulb on an open paperback book. "For reading," Phil said with a grin. "Bookcases," he added, and gestured to stones cantilevered on other stones.

Officer Ricardo patted a skin and walked

toward half of a Ping-Pong table balanced on handmade horses. He stopped. The table was covered with radio parts, knives, crayons, wires of all sizes, pliers, a buzzer, and a garter snake in a jar. He studied the big balloon with the camera strapped to it for aerial photographs.

"The invention table," Craig explained. The policeman went to the wall on which the serpentine water clock hung. He passed it by in favor of the uncovered assemblage of tubes, wires, condensers, and dials that was the pride of Batta.

The transmitter-receiver had been the devil to build, Craig went on. "Steve's uncle bought it and tried to assemble it. After he got through with it, it was a mess. He gave it to Steve. Only by reading off the directions thirteen times did we get it working."

Craig added, "Steve's soldering helped. The mess Johnny and I made on one connection took him a whole night to fix. But he stuck to it until it was right."

Steve plugged the transmitter-receiver into the battery and picked up the mike. Officer Ricardo turned and noticed the kitchen, a long plank with pots, pans, and a Sterno can. He walked over to the faucet that hung down from the ceiling on a pipe.

"Running water," said Phil. "Craig says we

should make a big Archimedes' water screw and wind the water out of the ground, but I like turning on faucets, even if I have to fill the can outside myself." He turned the handle. "Open the faucet, the water runs down the pipe from the can, and trickle, trickle into the pots and pans." It rasped and sputtered. "Whoops, out of water." Officer Ricardo laughed. He glanced into the pantry. Orange crates, hung above the kitchen table, were filled with thick plates and cups, cans of hash, french fried potatoes, beans, soup, and dog food.

"Who eats dog food?" he asked.

"That's Craig's. He feeds it to snakes, blue jays, and snails." Phil shoved Craig playfully. Craig swung at him.

"KX2ABC, KX2ABC, this is KX2BAT, this is KX2BAT. Blue Springs Police Department. This is Batta Command. KX2ABC, do you read me? Over." Steve threw the switch to the receiver. It yakked and sputtered. Officer Ricardo moved to his side. Craig stood beside him. He felt kindly toward the big officer who now shared their very lives, and he concentrated on the receiver as if his full attention would help it to speak.

"I guess we're out of range," Steve said and relaxed his spine. He sat up again. "KX2ABC,

KX2ABC. Calling Blue Springs Police Department. This is Batta Command. Do you read me? Over."

Craig nudged the anxious officer. "He's persistent," he whispered. "He'll get something."

"KX2ABC, this is KX2BAT Batta Command calling." Steve put his chin in his hands. "Let's add more antennas to broadcast farther. It's an FCC violation, because this set is for a thousand feet, but Mrs. Ricardo must be worried."

"Yeah, it's seven o'clock," said Phil glancing at the end wall.

Craig thought about his mother. He wondered whether she was worried.

"Let's eat," he finally said and took down a can of hash and a bottle of catsup.

"That's not enough," said Phil. "Better add some beans to it."

"I'm not hungry," Officer Ricardo said.

"Then maybe you'd like some raisins." Phil reached to the ceiling. He hand-over-handed a rope, and a basket came out of the darkness above the bunks. He reached into it. "Here," he said and gave Officer Ricardo a box of raisins and a bag of prunes. The officer put a prune in his mouth and studied the pulley that went from the kitchen table to the bunk. "For snacks?" he asked.

"Yeah, when we're resting."

"KX2ABC, this is KX2BAT." Craig listened to the flick of the switch. Static answered. "Durn," he heard Steve say. He lit the can of Sterno and placed it between two cinder blocks. Then he took down a pan and put it on the blocks so that the flames licked it.

Steve's voice spoke on and on. Suddenly a phrase of jazz music came in. Craig turned around. Steve had the jeweler's screwdriver and was carefully adjusting the tuner in the receiver.

"We're awfully close to Station Fourteen-fifty," Steve explained to the officer. Craig turned back to his job.

"Phil," he called presently, "you wanted a durn faucet, get some water in the tank. This stuff's like glue." Phil picked up a flashlight and bounded up the steps. In a few minutes his voice came out the faucet. "Turn the thing off!" he exclaimed, "or you'll all get drowned."

"KX2ABC, KX2ABC, this is KX2BAT, Blue Springs Police Department. This is Batta Command. Do you read me? Over."

9 SOS

At six-thirty that night Johnny was riding in the car with his father. The game of pitch was over. He was glad, for his father was cranky toward the end when he missed the curve balls and had to go down the big embankment after them. But they had joked and laughed, and his father now seemed pleased with himself. Johnny still thought they could have spent the afternoon to more purpose at the rocket site, but he guessed his father thought pitch was

Johnny's favorite pastime. He wondered how he could let him know he was interested in other things now. He had already told him so a hundred times, but somehow words were not enough. 'Sfunny thing, Johnny thought, how hard it is to get some perfectly obvious ideas across.

Suddenly he noticed the car had slowed down. Johnny looked out the window. Fog was obscuring the road. Then, as his father turned off the ridge and started down the hill to their house, they were plunged into what seemed like a glass of milk. The road was all but invisible. Johnny felt his dad's right leg quicken as his foot went on the brake.

"This is impossible!" Mr. Cooper said and eased the car down the hill. Carefully they crept around the bend and into the drive. They were both relieved when they were in the garage. The lights from the house shone warmly under the kitchen door. Johnny two-stepped it up the stairs and into the room.

"Hi, Mom," he called and threw his mitt across the kitchen, through the living room, and onto the Dutch sideboard.

"Johnny, stop it. This is not a stadium. Pick that up and *put* it away."

"I'm sorry." He skidded through the door before she could say anything else. But he need not have worried. Her attention was already on his father.

"John," she said, "tonight's the night we have that discussion with the children. We must discuss going to Aunt Mary's. Remember?"

"Oh, yes!" he said and washed his hands in the sink. "I enjoy these family discussions." He kissed her cheek. "It's a horrible night. I almost missed the drive and hit the mailbox."

"I'm glad you're home, dear," Mrs. Cooper said.

Johnny threw himself belly-first on the couch. Penny, his younger sister, screamed at him to get off her new jumper. He barely heard her for he was thinking of the rocket. However, his older sister Karen rushed to Penny's aid and shoved him to the floor. His father came into the room, sat down, and opened the newspaper. He read while the children argued. Suddenly the paper went down.

"Johnny," began Mr. Cooper. "This is the night we're going to discuss whether or not we go to Aunt Mary's for Columbus Day."

"Okay," Johnny said. "And then can we talk about coming to see the rocket? We've gotta have a committee to approve it, you know."

"Yes, I know. Mr. Brundage has called me. But, *you* know, afternoons and evenings are my busiest time in a town like this. Most of the committees have to meet when the men are home from work."

"Oh, sure, I know that."

Dinner was announced, and the Coopers sat down in silence. Mr. Cooper carved the lamb. When everyone was served he sat down quietly.

"Now, children," he said. "Let's have everyone's viewpoint on whether or not we visit Aunt Mary this Columbus Day."

"Okay," said Johnny brightly. "I don't want to go. I don't like just sitting around and doing nothin'."

"I don't want to go either," said Penny and cut her meat firmly.

"Me neither," said Karen.

"Now that's not a discussion," said Johnny's father firmly. "You've given opinions. We must have better reasons. More air."

"Well, frankly then," said Johnny, and he heard his voice weaken, "she always makes us rake leaves, or wash windows, or sit without making a mess. And that's hard to do."

"And you, Penny?" said Mr. Cooper with an edge of irritation.

"I think she's too old for me. She doesn't like frilly petticoats."

"Karen?"

"Well—" Johnny saw her glance at him for

courage. "If she wouldn't always make me keep my feet on the floor I might say yes. Would you tell her it's hard to keep your feet together on the floor when you're sitting? Then maybe I'll go."

Johnny saw his father put down his knife and fork. "Now, I've heard what you have to say. Let me speak. She's family, she's very old, and she loves you children."

"No she doesn't!" said Penny.

Johnny tried again. "Well," he said, "I think Penny is right, and I don't want to go."

"We must." Mr. Cooper picked up his knife and fork. Johnny dropped his.

"Go?"

"Yes."

"Has this been a discussion?"

"Yes."

"Well, then . . ." He hesitated. "I'm real mixed up about discussions. What I am trying to say is, why ask us? We'll go if we have to."

Johnny did not hear his father's answer. He had leaned back in his chair to think and had inattentively poked a forkful of lamb in his mouth. And then he heard a voice!

"—Batta Com—— Bat—— Com——ead me?" He sat up.

"Thanks, son"—his father was smiling again —"for your silent apology."

"—Batta ——ing Police ——ment." Johnny dug the fork further into the filling.

His father reached out and touched his hand. "I'm sorry. I don't mean to upset you, it's just that we *must* go to Aunt Mary's."

Johnny looked at him and wanted to say, "I'm not upset," but his tooth was talking.

He leaped up. "Dad," he said, "something's wrong. Something's wrong at Batta." The white fog swirled at the picture window. "Dad! I think Craig and Phil and Steve are calling for help. They're stuck in the fog."

"Help? What is this? Johnny, are you all right?"

Briefly he explained the tooth. Mr. Cooper pushed back from the table and rushed to the phone.

"Alice!" he said to Mrs. Brundage, "is Phil home?" He exchanged a few more exclamations, hung up, and called the Police Department. Johnny, still holding the fork on his tooth, followed him into the kitchen. After speaking briefly, his father turned to him. "What's their call number?"

"KX2BAT."

"KX2BAT." He listened and looked back at Johnny. "Is Officer Ricardo with them?"

"I don't know."

"He's missing and his wife is frantic."

"I'll bet he went out to see the rocket. Well, tell the chief he's okay. Tell them they have food, water, even electric lights. Tell them to try KX2BAT and they can talk to him." Johnny sat down on the kitchen stool as his father passed on his messages. Then Mr. Cooper hung up and they both waited in silence. Presently the phone rang again.

"Thank heavens," said Mr. Cooper. He turned to Johnny. "They're all fine!"

When he had put back the phone, Mr. Cooper surveyed Johnny.

"And now," he said, "let's have a real discussion. What *is* this Batta?"

10 THE PROTEST

Steve awoke first because Officer Ricardo had rolled over on him. He kicked Craig. Craig awoke.

"I'm hungry," he said.

"I'm sad," Steve whispered. "It was a great night. A really great night. But our secret's no more."

"Yeah," sighed Craig. "And now it's morning and we've gotta go home."

Steve lay silently.

"I'll go get the water," Craig finally said and stepped over Phil. He had no need to dress because he had never taken his clothes off. By the misty light coming in from a small window above the transceiver he found his way to the stairs. He walked outside.

The fog was lifting and the air smelled good. Craig took a deep breath. Tentative birds, confused by the mist, chirped sleepily in the bushes. Craig was amused for he realized they were uncertain as to whether to get up and face the bad weather or to clutch their night roosts tighter. He filled the galvanized can from the slow stream and went back to Batta.

Phil was cooking breakfast. Officer Ricardo was still sleeping, a great hunk of relaxation. "He had a pretty scary day," Craig observed to Phil.

Phil took down the four heavy plates and cups that Craig had made in school. "These are durn good," he said.

Craig picked up one of the cups and turned it over. "Miss Pierce sure wanted this to be an animal," he said. "She wanted a good exhibit for the PTA. But I didn't wanna make animals, 'cause we didn't have dishes for Batta. Still," he mused, "when I told her I really wanted to make dishes, she let me. She said something about art couldn't be dictated. 'Sfunny thing to say, don't you think, Phil?"

"I dunno. I get all mixed up about what they want you to do and what they don't. So I go along with them." He tilted and swirled the fry pan. "But I do know this much, hash is a durn sight easier to eat on your plates than on my ceramic giraffe."

They laughed.

Officer Ricardo awoke with a snort. He sat up and looked around, saw the boys, and grinned. "Good morning, good knights," he called. "I've always wanted a chance to say that." Everyone laughed.

Steve went to the sink to wash his face. As the cold water hit him he began to chuckle. He looked at the transmitter-receiver.

"All this fancy equipment," he said. "And Johnny gets us on a durn filling." Craig wondered about the possibilities of silver and mercury as he spooned out the food.

When the dishes were washed and put away, Craig, Phil, and Steve were ready to go. Officer Ricardo was not. He was contemplating the far wall and suggesting that a heating plant for winter might be installed there.

They waited for him, then walked up the steps. The sun had broken through the white mist.

"How're we gonna get home?" Officer Ricardo asked. "We have no gas."

"Paddle like geese," said Phil.

As the bulky swamp buggy inched along, the wheel dragging hard against their efforts, Phil suddenly pushed up on his elbows.

"Gee, it's Sunday," he said. "I'm gonna miss Dad's sermon if we don't hurry."

"Ya won't miss it," boomed Officer Ricardo, "if you paddle instead of back water."

Phil laughed at himself.

11 THE SPIDERLINGS

Two days after the fog-in Steve reported to Craig that Mr. Smith had gone to Europe. Steve joined the PTA dancing class, and Phil and Craig and Johnny signed up for the basketball team. Craig tried hard to develop "sportsmanship" and enjoy himself, especially after Johnny's father had told him that he should learn to compete when he was young, for he certainly would have to when he grew up. He could see how that might be true.

Nevertheless, he preferred to go to the island and learn the plants and watch the animals. The afternoons inventing gadgets at Batta with Phil and Johnny were restful and wonderful. This bothered him, for he did want to enjoy what he was supposed to.

A month passed.

Then Steve came into the school locker room one day shouting exuberantly that Mr. Smith was back. Craig relayed the good news to Phil and Johnny.

Three more days passed.

On the fourth day Craig called Officer Ricardo and asked tentatively whether the committee was ready to come to inspect the rocket.

"Craig," the officer sighed, "it's almost impossible to find a moment when one or the other of those men aren't busy." He paused. "And frankly, I've been busy, too."

"Oh, well," Craig heard himself say, "I understand. It's just that the weather is getting cold now, and the winter'll be hard on the rocket. If they don't inspect it soon, we'll never get 'er off."

"I know, Craig. Everyone wants to do what's best for you boys, believe me. Don't worry; the committee will get there."

Suddenly Craig wanted to go to the island. It had been a long time since he'd been there. The confusion of whether they had done something wonderful or something awful had dampened his interest in Batta. He noticed that the other boys were not so enthusiastic either, and, like him, they were all trying hard to take advantage of what the community offered. At this moment, however, nothing could replace the island and the ammunition shelter, the faucet and the bunks. It was Friday, and in half an hour the basketball team would play a practice game. Craig decided the heck with it. Today, at least, he was going to do what made him feel at ease with himself. Besides, the good players could stay in the whole game if he didn't show up. He pulled on a sweater and ran down the steps.

At the dock he made numerous tries before he started the long-idle swamp buggy. Eventually the engine caught and the craft plowed out among the cattails.

The island looked deserted. Leaves had fallen from the trees. Only seeds and berries remained. These, Craig thought, were not jubilant like the flowers and leaves, but hard and small—full of sleep and purpose. Craig opened a bittersweet berry and squeezed the yellow seed between his fingers.

He walked to the hollow where the raccoon slept. A bat hung inside the hole, upside down, and quiet. Suddenly a chickadee sang. It was a wistful call. The bird did not sound like spring although the notes were the same. He wondered why.

Slowly he sat down and crossed his ankles. His hand rested on a flat stone and idly he lifted it. White eggs of the ants clung to the underside, and a salamander slept, eyes open, too cold to know it had been disturbed. Craig put the stone back.

He felt better. He didn't feel rushed any more; and then, because everything around him was waiting, he decided that's how things were. Sometimes you had to wait.

Happily he stretched out in the leaves. A jimson weed, dried and angular, touched his cheek. He observed it casually, and then not so casually, for the tip was as active as a hive. He sat up. The jimson weed was covered with tiny spiders that had emerged in the warm sun. They were crawling over each other in an effort to get as high as they could on the gray-brown stalk. Craig concentrated on a single spider of the hundreds that moved so hastily.

The spiderling was pale and yellow, but determined. It attained the highest point on the weed and paused, turned its head into the autumn wind, and threw up its back feet. A thin thread of gossamer drifted out from its spinnerets. Craig rolled to his knees. The thread billowed in the breeze until it grew so long it had more strength than the spiderling. Then the spiderling let go and the thread bowed in the breeze and lifted the minute creature into the air. Craig stood up and saw the drifter turn and clutch its web with its front feet. It reefed in to the right as it sailed around a thistle. He followed the glitter of the sun on the web. It became entangled in a hackberry limb. The spiderling climbed it, reeling in its silk as it went. Then it turned its head into the wind again and spun out another balloon of thread. On this it rode out of sight.

"So that's how they get free," he said to himself. "They sail away and reel in their threads, sail away and reel in their threads."

Suddenly he knew that was what he was going to do, too. He jumped on the swamp buggy. It started immediately. Twenty minutes later Craig was running up the hill to his home when he saw his friend.

"Steve!" he called. "Hold it!"

The angular Steve turned, distributed his weight on both feet, and waited for his friend.

"Listen, I know how to get the rocket launched!" Craig gasped. "We sail away!" He drew a wide course with his arms. "We just sail to Batta and we reel in all the threads and wait."

"What are you talking about, Craig?"

"Well." He laughed at himself. "Let's go to the island tonight and not come back until the committee comes to find us. Let's just sit there until they look at the rocket."

"Well, I can't tonight."

"Why?"

"I'm going to the Soph Hop."

"Oh, well, just hop around for a few minutes. We'll wait for you."

"No, don't. I guess I'll stay all night."

"You mean you want to *dance?*" Craig asked incredulously. He couldn't believe what he had heard.

"Yes. I'm taking Cathy Smith to the dance, and I think I'll stay—and dance."

Craig stared. "But, Steve," he said, "we all said no girls, Steve. We promised we wouldn't bother with them."

"Well, it's different now," Steve said firmly.

"But, Steve!" Craig pleaded. "If we go out there—all of us—if we wait long enough . . . they'll come."

Steve turned away. "You fellows go. I won't tell."

Steve went up the road whistling. Craig clenched his fists and jabbed the air. Not Steve, he thought to himself. Not Steve. He can't let us down too. Then he was angry. He hurried home and called Johnny and Phil.

He was able to sway Johnny almost immediately, and Phil in about three animated sentences. They were going to wait at Batta until they got some action.

Craig threw a few things in a knapsack and ambled downstairs. His mother was working in the kitchen. "I'm going out," he called.

She called back, "Don't go far, dinner's almost ready."

He sauntered down the hill. The early November day smelled of walnuts and wild crab apples. The light was clear, the air warm. At last, he thought, we're going to do something about all this.

Phil, all grins and bravado, was at the wharf when he got there. "My folks are gonna blow their tops," he said and threw his sack onto the swamp buggy. "I may stay forever. On the other hand," and Phil's voice sounded forlorn, "they may not even miss me. They're going to a meeting tonight."

Johnny snapped the dry joe-pye weed stems as he jumped off the road and ran down the path. He was in a fine mood, braces gleaming behind his smile, arms swinging loosely. He jumped on the swamp buggy.

"Hey," Phil said as Craig started the engine, "where's Steve?"

Craig turned his back and yanked the cord. His anger came back to him. "He's got a girl!" he shouted.

"You're kidding!" Phil said. "Not Steve. Steve's gonna be a real scientist."

"Well, he isn't now. He's taking Cathy Smith to a dance."

Craig put the engine in gear. Phil and Johnny were too stunned by the news to say any more. After a time Johnny shrugged, looked toward the island, and shouted, "To shreds with them all! And now to victory!" The craft sailed out beyond the reeds and across the sleeping waters of the slow stream.

They ate an early dinner and wandered outside to look at the rocket. "She's beautiful," said Craig admiringly. "She's just right!"

"She's gotta go off," said Phil, then added, "and she will!"

Briefly they wrestled in the grass, then picked the leaves out of the command station and launching pit. Finally Craig gathered a tin can of hickory nuts. He cracked them and passed them around, occasionally contemplating a frog pressing itself into the mud for winter.

When it grew dark and he could no longer see, Craig sat up in the grass and looked toward the town. "I don't hear any sirens," he said. "I wonder if they know we're missing?"

Phil listened. The wind sang in the hemlocks and tapped the dry willow limbs together. "Let's turn on the receiver. We can listen to the news broadcasts about us."

Down inside Batta Craig felt a little sorry for himself as the four lights lit the bunks and bounced off the chrome of the receiver. He wasn't even missed.

Phil dialed the local radio station. There were no station breaks for an emergency, no frantic bulletins. Craig walked to the invention table, picked up one of the short-range walkie-talkies assembled from kits, and flipped it on.

Johnny changed the battery in another. He said they were going to need them to talk to each other when everybody came out to launch the rocket and he wanted his perfect.

The news came on. They rushed to the transceiver. The Security Council of the U.N. was meeting, a local man had won some award, and the Blue Springs football team had lost a game. Craig listened intently until a commercial came on, then he turned down the volume.

"What time is it?" he asked.

Phil walked to the far wall and contemplated the convoluted water clock that hung there. "It's stopped," he said and glanced at his watch. "Seven o'clock. Too soon to be missed, I guess."

He picked up the glass cylinder on which were marked the minutes and hours and emptied the water into the bottle reservoir near the ceiling. He left enough water in the cylinder to read seven o'clock, then replaced it at the mouth of the twisted and looped glass tubing. He watched a drop of water leave the reservoir and make its way around and down the labyrinth. It fell into the cylinder. A second later another drop followed it. The clock began to drip off the seconds and minutes.

Phil contemplated his creation. He had made it at home last winter, sitting for twelve hours to check it with the electric clock on the wall. When the drip was perfect, he had gingerly carried the whole contraption to Batta where everyone had helped him secure it to the wall. It was a great success, and off and on during the past year as they had sat at the worktable, some one would make suggestions for improving the glass wonder. They were only suggestions, however. The clock was splendid just as it was.

When it was set, Phil joined Craig and

Johnny on the bunks. Craig ran his fingers over the book collection. Nothing appealed to him. "Let's make comic books," he said. "We haven't made any in a long time." Johnny thought that was the only thing to do and got out notebooks and pencils.

He licked the point of his pencil and said, "Think I'll do another episode of MXIGR Smith." He began to draw. Craig watched him. "I'm gonna do Steve, the Ladykiller." No one laughed.

"Do some more about the bean factory in Andromeda," said Phil. "That's not so irritating."

Craig watched Phil draw a balloon to the mouth of a fish, then ran his hand over the open page and went to work.

An hour passed. The news came on again. They jumped from the bunk to listen. It was almost a repeat of the seven o'clock news. The boys returned morosely to the bunk.

"You'd think someone would have looked in the tub by now," said Phil. "The last thing I said was that I was gonna take a bath."

"Yeah," mumbled Johnny. "You might be drowned. And who'd care?"

The water clock dripped on. Johnny fished the basket of food to his bunk and took out some crackers.

"Time to exchange," Craig said and everyone yawned, stretched, and passed the books around.

"Ha, ha!" Johnny roared.

Craig leaned over his shoulder to see what he had done to make Johnny laugh. "What's funny?"

Johnny pointed to the heroine, a worker in the Andromeda bean factory. She was dressed for a dance, her chipmunk face frowning, her starfish body struggling against the upside-down position that weightlessness had caught her in. Her balloon read, "I'll never be able to dance with that divine Steve, the foreman, if I don't find my antidrifting rocket."

"Serves her right," said Johnny.

"Wait'll you see the rest," Craig chuckled. "Turn the page."

Johnny turned the page and rolled onto his arm with laughter. She had drifted against an ellipse, one of the curved lines that made up her house. "Help!" she was saying. "I'm stuck on the locus of all the points, the sum of whose distances from two fixed points are called 'foci.'"

"That's great." He laughed harder.

Craig turned happily back to Phil's book. Presently he began to laugh. "Howdidja think of this spy outfit—American Unit for Nosecone Tracking?"

Phil rolled his tongue against his cheek. "Like all those big agencies get their names. First I thought of a word—aunt—then I fitted the names to it."

Craig glanced at his friend and grinned. "You've got insight."

"Johnny," Phil said after a pause, "I like this part where MXIGR plans a helium camp-out during the International Year of the Quiet Sun. Nice thought." They finished and exchanged. Finally everyone had read everything. Johnny rolled onto his back. "Let's go outside," he suggested. "Maybe we can hear the police sirens and see the searchlights."

"Yeah," said Phil enthusiastically. "That's it. They're still searching and don't want to broadcast the news until they find us."

" 'Course," answered Craig and followed the racing Johnny up the steps and into the moonless night. But there were no searchlights above the town, only a dome of stars and a single plane blinking into the suburban airport.

"Didja hear something?" whispered Johnny. "Listen!"

There was a quack in the night, followed by the beat of wings on the water. "Snapping turtle after a duck," Craig said. "No," said Johnny. "Not that—the siren sound." Craig listened harder. A far-away note reached his ears. "Night heron," he answered.

"Oh."

Craig jumped for a dark branch and swung on it. Phil picked up a stone under his foot and threw it over the water. It took a long time to plop.

"Aw, let's go to bed," Johnny said. "We'll need our wits in the morning when the committee comes."

As Craig crawled onto his bunk he moved too vigorously. His foot struck Johnny's back.

"Quit it!" Johnny shouted and struck him.

Craig hit him back. "What's eatin' you? I didn't mean to."

"Aw, you're always actin' like a blundering bear or some nature thing," Johnny muttered irritatedly.

"Oh, shut up!" yelled Phil. "We may be here for a long, long time. You'd better not start fighting now."

Craig switched out his light and put his head down. Johnny's light went out, then Phil's. He listened to the drip of the water clock until he finally fell asleep.

12 THE DECISION

Saturday morning did not dawn in underground Batta, so the boys slept late. Craig was startled to consciousness when he nearly rolled off the bunk. "Hey! It's late." He stood up. "The water clock's stopped." It had dripped to seven and emptied the reservoir. It was 8:15 by his watch. He awoke Phil, who jumped down from the rock and sleepily poured enough water in the reservoir to reset it. "Eight-seventeen!" he bellowed. "Everybody up!" Craig hopefully turned on the receiver. A commercial extolled the virtues of a shampoo.

Johnny opened his eyes. "Any news?"

"No," said Phil. "Not even a siren." He lit the stove. "I think they're all so busy they still don't know we're gone."

Johnny was washing his face. "It sure doesn't make you feel very important, does it?" he said. "Let's go up and see." He ran up the stairs.

Craig hopped behind him.

The morning was bright and clear. A flock of crows screamed fiercely as they chased a marsh hawk across the water. He listened to the blackbirds chirp peacefully along the marsh edge. "No one's beating the bushes," he said. "The birds are too calm."

"Boy, nobody cares a hoot, do they?" said Phil.

"They sure don't."

"They wouldn't even care if we shot the durn rocket. They wouldn't even know."

"No, they wouldn't," agreed Johnny vehemently.

"They just don't care," said Craig, "so why don't we set it off?"

There was a long pause. Phil turned slowly to Craig. "Yeah—why don't we set it off? We're never gonna get permission anyway. Who's to know?"

"No one."

"Fellows," said Johnny, "this is it!"

"Yeah," Craig said thoughtfully. "This *is* it!"

Johnny ran for the equipment box, Phil went into Batta for the battery to spark the ignition panel. Craig rolled back the covering on the rocket and checked its angle of fire. He took a countdown sheet out of the equipment box and laid it on the ground before him. "T-minus twelve," he began nervously. "You know, this isn't our latest countdown. Steve's got the new one." Phil looked over his shoulder. "Oh, well, it'll work, and it's less elaborate. Let's use it."

The three boys worked quietly getting the parts in order. Suddenly the silence was ended by a blast of sound.

"Boys, are you there? Boys, are you there? This is Chief Nelson." The voice was amplified by a battery megaphone.

Slowly Craig stood up and stared at Johnny. "Now whatta we do?"

"This is it!" said Johnny grimly. "The dickens with 'em."

Craig worked faster. Phil secured the wires to the ignition panel.

"Boys, are you there?"

Johnny took the engines out of their wrappings.

"I'll read the countdown," shouted Craig.

"T-minus twelve. Pack flameproof recovery wadding into the body tube. Insert the parachute . . . or . . ." he turned to the others, "the Batta banner. Do we have time for that?"

"No," said Phil.

"*Boys!*" The voice was a woman's, Phil's mother. "*This is ridiculous. Are you there? Phil, come in this minute.*" Phil took a few steps toward the voice, then Craig saw him gather his courage and step back.

"T-minus eleven," Craig shouted. "Insert engines."

Johnny placed the twenty-four engines in position.

"*Craig! John! Phil.*" It was Steve's voice. "*Come in. The committee will meet. If you're coming in give a blast on the transistor. If not, give two.*"

Johnny picked up the small radio and glanced at his friends. "Is it two?"

"It's two!" shouted Phil.

"This afternoon's too late," snapped Craig. "Besides, looking at it doesn't mean they'll let us put it off."

"Right!" Phil answered.

Johnny turned the transistor radio as high as it would go. It let out a jazzy wail. He turned it down. A second later he turned it up again. Craig got out the payload.

"All right, boys." It was Mr. Brundage. *"We'll give you a count to ten, then we're coming out."*

Craig sensed Phil hesitate, but Johnny dusted off the microclips. "T-minus ten. Check microclips," Craig shouted.

The megaphone on shore blared, *"One, two, three . . ."*

Craig picked up the safety code. "I will launch my rocket," he read, "using a launching rail system or other suitable guide means aimed within twenty-five degrees of the vertical to assure a safe and predictable flight path, and will launch only those rockets whose stability characteristics have been predetermined." He turned to Phil. "Are we okay?"

"Guess so."

"Four, five . . ."

"T-minus nine. Install the nose cone or payload section. Check the condition of payload. Did we?"

"Sorta," replied Johnny.

"Six, seven, eight . . ."

Johnny kneeled in front of the rocket, clips in his hands, waiting for the next count.

"Nine, ten! We're coming out."

Craig stopped the count as the roar of a motorboat stood him on his feet. He lifted the paper to his face, "T-minus eight. Install michrome igniter in the first-stage engines." He heard the boat coming nearer.

"It's go," whispered Johnny and ran to the command center to get behind the barricade. Craig glanced at the shore and followed him.

"T-minus seven," he read nervously. "Clear the area, check for low-flying aircraft. Alert recovery crew and trackers." He scanned the sky. Nothing was in sight but a low-flying crow beating west of the spruce trees. "I'll hafta be recovery crew and tracker," he said. "Durn Steve for getting messed up with a girl. There's a lota work to this."

"Aw, we can do it," said Johnny. "We've practiced a hundred times."

"T-minus six." Craig saw the motorboat through the willows. Four men and Steve were in it. He read on. "Arm the launch panel!"

Johnny's hand trembled slightly as he put the key into the ignition switch. Then the speed of the boat motor was checked for a landing.

"T-minus five." Craig reached for the alti-scope under the shelf. He remembered that originally they planned to check the altitude of the flight with this instrument. He placed it near him.

"Wonder where they got the motorboat?" he said.

"Doesn't matter. 'Stoo late," shouted Phil.

"T-minus four.

"T-minus three."

"Hold!" shouted Johnny. "They're coming to the island through the range area." Craig waited. He heard the boat bump the wharf.

"They're okay now," shouted Johnny.

Feet sounded on the wharf, voices rose, and Steve broke into the meadow on a dead run.

"Watch it!" Craig shouted. "T-minus two!"

Steve ran on. His face was angry. "Don't you dare!" he shouted. "Don't!" He leaped past the rocket and skidded into the command center.

"Are you crazy? You're gonna spoil everything. They've come out to inspect it!"

Craig saw Johnny's hand drop from the switch, and he slowly crumpled the countdown sheet. Phil said shakily, "Is my dad here?"

"Yes, and yours too, Johnny. And Mr. Smith and Officer Ricardo."

"Now whattawegonna do?" asked Phil.

"Take that thing apart while I divert the committee," snapped Steve.

"How are you gonna divert them?" asked Johnny, his voice wavering.

"With Batta! I'm gonna have to show them Batta while you get that rocket disassembled." He turned away angrily and ran toward the men who were lingering along the path, looking at the trails and buildings. Steve stopped and called back, "And I don't want to, but you guys have asked for it." He stormed away.

Slowly Craig and Johnny unhitched the wires. Phil took the engines out of their casings. Through the woods Craig heard Steve say, "I think you'll understand what we've done if you come this way first."

13 THE COMMITTEE

The rocket was disassembled, the parts returned to their boxes. Craig sat down on the edge of the launch pit and put his chin in his hands. The excitement had drained him and he felt tired. Phil apparently felt the same way for he took a deep breath and pushed back his damp curls. "And now, for my father," he said weakly.

"I think we're in trouble," said Johnny.

"We can still get in the swamp buggy and get

out of here," said Phil. "There's a train north at eleven o'clock."

"Let's," said Johnny, and he jumped to his feet. Craig folded and unfolded his arms. "What I can't understand—" he was not listening to the new plan "—is what's so wrong about what we've done. We've only built a rocket and tried to get someone to approve it so we can put it off."

Phil sat down. "Yeah, what've we done?"

"We haven't done anything," said Johnny. "So what're we afraid of?"

"Nothing," said Phil. He stood up, but his shoulders did not straighten. Slowly he walked toward Batta.

Craig and Johnny followed him. The door to Batta stood ajar. A blue jay sat upon it, cracking a nut.

Halfway down the steps, Craig hesitated. The room below was ominously silent. But it was too late to turn back. Slowly he followed Phil.

"Hi, son!" said Mr. Brundage brightly, his great figure curled to avoid the ceiling. "This is some gadget you made." He pointed to the water clock. Craig could see that Phil was relieved. He grinned, then walked slowly toward his clock.

Craig glanced at Officer Ricardo and Johnny's

father. Neither seemed angry, he thought. In fact, Officer Ricardo had an I-told-you-so look on his face. He was rocking on his toes. Craig studied Mr. Smith. He, too, looked pleased.

"One problem with it," Phil said to his father, "is that it needs an alarm to wake me up when it runs out of water at night. But I think I know how to do it." He was talking fast. "I'm gonna put a wooden spool in the reservoir; like this, with a string tied to it and two paper clips on the end of the string. As the water falls, the spool falls; but the paper clips come up. They hit a copper circuit when the thing's empty. The circuit's gonna be connected to a buzzer. It'll go off and wake me up."

"That sounds good," Mr. Brundage said. "I think that ought to work beautifully." He turned to Johnny's father with a prideful grin. "Don't you?"

Johnny's father nodded and picked up a walkie-talkie. He flicked it on. Johnny took another and said, "Hi," then switched it off.

"The boys made these," Johnny's father said to Mr. Brundage. He nodded. Soon every man was asking questions and as they did, the story of Batta unrolled: its discovery, its evolution.

Phil expounded. "One day," he said, "Craig was fooling around with a bunch of snails and discovered they spun little threads as they walked under the water. He was sorta crazy about environments then—on changing the environment of animals to see if *they* would change—and he wondered if the snails would spin at a high altitude. That got Steve to thinkin' and he suggested we build a rocket and shoot them up there and find out."

"Sounds more like a weed growing than anything dangerous," said Mr. Cooper. "Let's have a look at this controversial instrument."

The men filed out of Batta and walked in good spirits to the rocket. Steve took over and explained the details, speaking mainly to Mr. Smith, who was interested in the command center and the launching pit.

"Nice design," Mr. Smith said of the rocket. "It's original, isn't it? I've not seen one like it."

"Sort of. It's a copy of Titan Three."

When Steve had finished showing off the rocket, the men sat down in the meadow and began to talk. The conversation rambled from how beautiful the island was to the rules and regulations about rockets. Craig listened, growing impatient. No one was talking about setting it off. Finally he *had* to ask:

"Well, can we launch her?"

A silence followed. He was on his belly and he rolled to his knees and stared at the men.

"I guess what's bothering me, Craig," said

Mr. Brundage, "is really two things. A scientist I talked to in Albany said there's always a risk in these things no matter how perfect they are; and"—he cleared his throat—"I don't like being forced."

"Forced?" said Phil. "Whattaya mean?"

"I mean, your running away from home and scaring us to death to force us out here. I don't think this is the proper way to handle things."

Craig slumped in misery. The minister, of course, was right. They had done exactly that. He wanted to say that it at least got them out there, but he felt that was not quite the right thing to say, so he remained quiet. So did Phil, Steve, and Johnny. There was nothing to argue about. If they had been wrong, that was that.

"Well, let's talk it over," said Mr. Cooper. "I feel a little pressured, too."

Officer Ricardo started to say something but apparently changed his mind. "Let's get back," he said. "I've gotta get to work."

The last words Craig heard as the men boarded the motorboat were Mr. Smith's. "Maybe we can clear this up," he said. "They *have* done an admirable job." But the roar of the engine choked the answer.

"Let's cover the rocket and go," said Steve. He pulled in the swamp buggy and grabbed the nearest paddle.

14 THE INTERVAL

Craig waited. He felt too discouraged all week to visit the island. Sunday came and went without a mention of the rocket, then Monday, Tuesday, Wednesday—the week. He saw the weather change from the bright clearness of Indian summer to the gray-blue of late autumn, and he knew that the island in the marsh was as cold as the November air. He imagined leaves blowing, grass bending over beneath the trees. Only the sturdy pipsissewa and the hemlocks, he thought, were green, and he realized that by now the wind had filled the launching pit with leaves and jammed the wings of thistle seeds into the command center. It would shove broken stems under the door to Batta and shake the hemlock needles over the rocks above the subterranean room.

Friday morning he looked out his window and knew the winter had sealed the island in sleep. The raccoon and the chipmunks would be dozing, the crickets would come into the shelter of Batta.

Saturday passed without a word from the committee.

On Monday, down the hill and beyond the marsh the school bell rang to call the students to classes. Craig was still on the athletic field when he heard it. He ran to make the deadline, swung through the oaken doors, and burst upon Steve and Cathy. Steve was carrying her books.

" 'Scuse me!" he blurted and hurried past them in embarrassment. From a safe distance he looked back and saw Steve grinning happily as he held the inner door open for the young lady with straight black hair that bounced against her slim neck. Craig looked away. He could not understand why Steve smiled. She combed her hair too much, she snickered and laughed with the other girls too much. On the whole, he thought, she was about as interesting as a mop and a bucket.

He strode down the hall. Fortunately Phil and Johnny were ahead of him and Craig forgot the ruined Steve as he saw them. "Phil!" he called. "Has your dad changed his mind?"

Phil slumped expressively. "He's working on a play with the church drama group. I haven't seen Dad to really talk to him since the sit-out."

Craig hit his books with his fist. Johnny blew his breath out slowly and loudly. The three climbed the steps to their homeroom. As they turned at the landing, Craig saw Steve and Cathy again. Steve was laughing with her, his hand on her shoulder. The three boys exchanged glances and hurried ahead.

Tuesday passed, then Wednesday. At midnight on Thursday Craig heard his radio buzz. He heard it first in a dream. In the dream he was tied in a web of ropes, being yanked over a field of flowers. Many people were pulling on the ropes, some he didn't even know. He was thoroughly frightened. Then Cathy came over the field and sat down at a machine. She began to spin. The machine whirred and buzzed. The noise went on and Cathy kept smiling and holding up the rope she was making. With a jump of fright Craig woke up. Shaking, he stared at the dark ceiling. The whirr and buzz sounded again. He laughed with relief. It was his radio. Rolling to his belly, he opened the switch and fumbled for the mike. "Craig to Steve, whatdaya want?" he said sleepily. "Over."

"Steve to Craig. I've just come in from a date. Cathy said her father had called the committee together. They're gonna meet Friday and decide something. Over."

"Swell. Wonderful. Great. Over. Over and out!" Craig leaped back into bed and pounded the pillow with excitement. He thought about the snails and where to find some new ones for the payload. They had been left out ten days ago in the rush to get the rocket launched. Now he could think about them again; but instead, he fell asleep. He did not dream.

On Friday Craig blasted his saxophone through band practice, then he ran all the way home and down to the cellar for his hip boots. Before sundown he was wading at the edges of the marsh, gathering the winter-retreating water snails. They were black and spiraled. Their feet were pulled high up in the shells. He carried them home and put them in the bathroom sink, with a trickle of water running to give them oxygen. In the warmth of the bathroom they began to crawl, and when he reached his hand into the water, he could feel the invisible threads of mucus they spun as they moved. He watched one stop. Its shell lifted as it ate its trail again.

He wondered what they would do at two thousand feet.

Friday evening was long. Craig stayed near the telephone. But the telephone did not ring. A flock of swans flew over the house, crying their recognition notes as they maneuvered the cloudy sky, and a fox called from the ridge. Slowly the hands on the clock moved around until it was morning.

Craig called Steve. Steve called Johnny. Johnny called Phil. Phil called Craig. His voice stayed on one note as he excitedly announced that the committee had met, and might let them put off the rocket, but they weren't sure. Craig called Steve.

Then it was Sunday and Monday again.

On Tuesday afternoon Craig joined his friends on the wharf at Rushing Road. It was cold and the first snow of the season was falling. The thin flakes slipped off the limbs of the trees and melted on the ground. A few hung on Steve's dark eyelashes, but they, too, disappeared when they touched his skin. Phil checked the tank of the swamp buggy. "We're out of gas," he said.

"And we've got no money," added Johnny. "I guess we've had it. I guess we might as well go home and join the world. We'll polish our shoes and go to dancing class and Boy Scouts, and school sports and paddle tennis and—"

"Write book reports and bibliographies," added Phil.

"Steve," said Craig, trying to control his voice, "you should've let us put the rocket off. You shouldn't have stopped us. Now we'll never see 'er go."

"Yeah, Steve," agreed Phil. "I think we've had it. I'm still for launching 'er. Who'll know?"

"We can't," said Steve firmly. "I've given Mr. Smith the engines to check out."

"Well, let's get 'em back," Craig said. "You get 'em back, you know him best."

"I can't," Steve mumbled.

"Why not?"

" 'Cause, he's busy."

"So what? We're your best friends."

"It's different. Mr. Smith is trying to help us, it's just that . . ."

"Nobody cares," boomed Johnny and picked up a stone. He skipped it across the water.

"No," Steve mused, "it's not that, I don't think. It's something else. Something else is bothering everybody and I don't know what it is."

Craig looked at his watch. "It's four o'clock. I've gotta go home." He jumped for a tree limb and swung on it. Dropping lightly, he trotted down the path. At the road he turned and came back. "Steve, if you'd stop running around with girls, things would be all right. We could do it!" He was hurt and furious at everyone and everything. He kicked a tree.

Johnny turned to Steve. "He's right. You've chickened out on us all because of a girl!"

Steve's eyes narrowed. "I don't like that, John." He shoved the boy's shoulder. Johnny swung his fist. It struck Steve across the face. Steve punched him back and jumped on him. Their fists thudded against chins and chests.

Phil stepped back to watch the fight. Craig came closer. He wanted to punch someone, too. He felt frustrated and disappointed in everyone. Suddenly Phil rushed Steve and Johnny and shoved them into the water with his shoulder. They went under, then struggled to their feet, wet and angry. They stared at Phil. They stared at each other. Johnny felt a lump in his throat. "The dickens with all of you!" he cried, climbed ashore, and ran home through the woods.

Steve crawled up on the wharf, slowly, his rage obvious. He stood right in front of Phil and with a powerful swing punched him hard in the chest. "This is it! I'm through!" he cried.

Phil curled over. He grabbed his ribs. The tears welled in his eyes, and Craig, unable to watch him cry, turned and ran.

It wasn't until the next morning that Craig learned that Phil had broken a rib. The dean called him and Steve and Johnny into his office and told them. Steve sank into the nearest chair and put his head in his hands.

"How did it happen?" the dean asked. "Apparently Phil won't tell his parents."

Steve looked up. "We got in a fight. I socked him." He lowered his head again. "It's the rocket," he whispered. "It's the dumb, foolish rocket. I wish we'd never built it."

The dean lectured them for a few minutes on friendship and sent them back to their classes. Craig took the back stairs to his homeroom. He didn't want to see the others. There was nothing left.

15 THE TEACHER

Thanksgiving came. Craig stopped by to see Phil, but felt too guilty to stay more than a few minutes. He played the last football game, went to the Sports Banquet and listened while the best players got awards. Johnny went with his family to his Aunt Mary's again. Steve saw less and less of Cathy. He didn't touch the radios or go to Batta, and the wind blew over the island in the marsh and froze the ground around the rocket.

On a snowy December afternoon Craig was walking down the corridor of the second floor of the school by himself when he saw Johnny coming toward him. Noticing that the door to Mr. Brian's science lab was open, he slipped in. "Can I help you?" The teacher was putting away Bunsen burners.

"Sure, come in."

Mr. Brian's red hair began far back on his forehead and his eyes drooped slightly. His rounding waist gave a mature contour to the energetic figure. Mr. Brian unhitched a Bunsen burner and wrapped the rubber tubing around it, while Craig disconnected a burner, blew into its sooty pipe, and carried it to the cabinet.

"I haven't seen you with your friends lately," Mr. Brian said. "Did something happen?"

Craig found the question hard to answer. He walked quietly to the lab table and picked up another Bunsen burner. "Yes," he said. It was a curt answer that implied, "Period. Don't go on." He put the burner away.

Fifteen minutes passed. Mr. Brian went to his desk. Craig glanced at him from time to time.

Finally he made a wide circle of the lab, remembering the teakettle, the experiments in mixing chemicals, the lecture on aeronautics. He could stand his inside ache no longer. He walked across the room to the teacher's desk.

"I've got to talk to someone," he said. "Everybody's so durn miserable."

Mr. Brian put down his pencil. He smiled. "It seems so," he said.

Craig fingered a paperweight. "At first I thought it was because of Cathy and the fight, and because Phil got hurt. But that isn't it. Heck, we weren't all mad at each other the day we sawed Johnny out of a tree and broke his leg. I dunno what's the matter, do you?"

"As a matter of fact, I've been thinking about it. I think I do."

"It's the rocket, isn't it?" Craig welled out. "It's the rocket and all the parents that want to be our buddies. They say they want to help us, but they don't, do they?"

"They can't."

"Why?"

"They're parents, not buddies, not teachers, not best friends—but parents."

Craig frowned and tried to understand.

"When parents get into roles—like buddies, teachers, doctors, psychologists—they get confused and don't know what to do."

Craig thought about that. "You mean parents act differently toward their kids than teachers do?"

"Shouldn't they?" Mr. Brian picked up his

pencil. His hand moved swiftly over an exam, checking the trues and falses. Craig listened to the soft sound of the lead.

"Well, then," he said slowly, "I know what to do." Mr. Brian glanced up.

"You're a teacher. We run experiments in the lab. Why can't we run one outdoors? Could you make the rocket a class project?" He watched Mr. Brian's face as the teacher put his pencil down and folded his arms.

"Yes, I could," Mr. Brian said. "Yes, that would make sense."

"Will you?" Craig grabbed the desk. "Will you do it?"

"Why not? I'd have to be filled in on your plans and the instruments you're using," Mr. Brian said. "But you and Phil and Steve and Johnny could help me. In fact, you could lecture on its construction to the whole class."

Craig described the three stages and the kind of engines they were using.

"Hold on. Let's have it all tomorrow," Mr. Brian said. "I'll turn over the class to you fellows."

"Okay." Craig rushed for his books, adjusted them against his side, and threw his back against the door.

"This is so simple," he said.

"Two more things," Mr. Brian said. "I'll call

Mr. Brundage and see if it's all right with his committee if I take this over. Is that okay?"

"I guess so," Craig said. "But it kinda scares me. Maybe there's another principle involved here, like going over people's heads, or something like that."

Mr. Brian laughed. "I don't think so. They're all anxious to find the best way to solve this."

"Oh sure," Craig finally agreed. "And the other thing?"

"I understand the engines need to be approved. How can I get them?"

"Mr. Smith has them. Maybe if you called him he'd give *you* an okay." Craig turned to leave. He came back. "By the way, I can understand now why our parents couldn't decide this matter; but why couldn't Mr. Smith? Why couldn't he approve it?"

"Aw, come on, Craig. Haven't you heard? Cathy doesn't want her boyfriend blowing himself sky-high."

"I see," said Craig. "So that's it!" He made a wry face and pushed through the door.

16 THE ROAD OUT

At five o'clock that same night Steve was in his room painting the walls. He had no desire to see his friends or Batta, so when his mother mentioned that his room needed repainting he had offered to do it. He knew that concentrating on getting a brushful of paint against the wall without dripping it would help take his mind off the whole confusing autumn.

He moved carefully down the west wall

where the transceiver sat. The circuit was still open, though no messages had come over it since the fight. He thought he might as well turn it off and disconnect it. He could do a better paint job if it were removed. He climbed down the ladder and walked to the receiver.

"Craig to Steve. Craig to Steve. Over."

Steve was startled at the sudden blare. For a moment he stared at the receiver. Then he smiled. It was good to hear the familiar voice again. He almost tripped as he ran to his transmitter, picked up the microphone, and switched the button to broadcast. "Steve to Craig. Hi! Over."

"Craig to Steve. Mr. Brian is going to help us put the rocket off. We're gonna get to Zero after all!" Steve sat down on his bed and grinned as he listened to the description of Craig's discussion with Mr. Brian. The story ended as his friend said, "So get the scale drawings and data of the Batta booster, and bring them to school tomorrow with a speech. Over."

"Roger, over and out!" Steve switched off his speaker, closed the bucket of paint, ran to the basement, and washed out the brush. "So one wall's yellow and the others are green," he said as he dashed up the flight of stairs three at a time and over to his files. He took out a folder marked "Batta Booster" and spread out the drawings, measurements, and a photograph of the Titan III rocket which had inspired the design.

He refreshed his mind on the construction. Each tube, he recalled, was two and a quarter inches in diameter. He studied the first-stage rockets. There were six tubes, fifteen inches high, including the nose cones that Phil and Mr. Brundage had carved. He chuckled as he recalled how that had only been a whittling demonstration.

"The six first-stage rockets," he said aloud in his best lecture tone, "surround the thirty-two-inch second and third stages." He thought he ought to explain how an inner tubing extended down an inch to make a snug connection between stages two, three, and the payload capsule. He rehearsed the description.

Now, he thought, how do I tell them about the engines? "There are three engines apiece," he said out loud, "in the six first-stage boosters. Each has a three-point-five-pound thrust, giving a total thrust of sixty-three pounds." He thought that was wordy but went on, "The second stage has two rocket engines with twenty pounds of thrust. They give a thrust of forty pounds.

"And students," he said to the yellow wall, "the third stage has four three-point-five-pound rocket engines with a thrust of fourteen pounds." It was going easily now. Then he thought about the payload. He flipped through the stack of papers. The payload design was missing, together with the measurements for the test tube, two rocket engines, and transistor-transmitter that would beep back the where-abouts of the capsule when it came down. He found the diagrams of the wire that bound the first-stage boosters to the second stage, but no capsule. He switched on his speaker and picked up his mike.

"Steve to Craig."

"Craig to Steve. Whatcha want? I'm busy. I'm trying to figure out the nichrome-clip as-sembly—the one that goes from the first-stage engines to the ignition panel. Did we ever diagram this? Over."

"Yes. Johnny has it. He took it the day we rehearsed the wiring. I'm looking for the pay-load drawing. Do you have it? Over."

"Phil's got it. He wants to tell about that tomorrow, but not the experiment or banner. That's still a secret, Steve, okay? Over."

"Okay! Over."

"By the way, Johnny's writing notes to the committee inviting them to Batta D-day, T-time. He wants to know if this Saturday is all right? Over."

"Wait. I'll look at the calendar. Hold." Steve leaned over the schedule on his desk. He returned to the mike. "Saturday, December the fourteenth—and I'd say eleven A.M.—is perfect for me. Mr. Brian can get this stuff in a minute. It's simple. Besides, he already knows most of it; the theory, that is, and that's the might of it. The practical stuff is as simple as assembling a flashlight. Over."

"I'll check the date with Mr. Brian," Craig said. "Hey, Steve, know what Johnny said when I told him about Mr. Brian helping? He said, 'Craig, you've thought good, and found us a man in the twentieth century.' That Johnny's a nail-hitter." He was about to say "Over," but thought of something else. "And hey, Steve, you know what Mr. Brundage said when Mr. Brian called him? He said, 'I abdicate to the institution and the brilliant maneuver of the boys. It's go.' How about that? Over."

"Well, now the only road out is up. Time everyone realized it. Over and out."

Steve worked through his dinner, a pizza which he ate on the floor. He went to bed feeling light and maneuverable again. Even his feet clicked together as he dove for the sheets.

Just as he was falling asleep, Craig's voice came over the radio. "Craig to Steve. Do you think the committee will come? Over."

"Steve to Craig. I doubt it. They're awfully busy, you know. Over and out."

The next morning Craig met his friends at their lockers. Each had a folder in his hands. They talked fast and excitedly, then ran up the steps and down the tile-lined corridor to the science lab. Mr. Brian had not arrived. They laid out their notes and diagrams and swung to the door. Craig jumped for the top of the doorsill, Johnny jumped after him. "I feel as if the molasses is out of me," he said. "This is a fine day."

Craig was aware that Phil did not jump. "How're your ribs?" he asked quietly.

"Ya can't kill a good man," Phil bragged.

"That's right," Steve said.

The lecture began at second period. As Steve began to speak, Craig noticed with some pride that Mr. Brian had a pencil and notebook. Steve opened the lecture by describing the layout of Batta, the launch pit, command station, and observation bunker. Mr. Brian listened intently. So did the class.

Then Craig got up, cleared his throat, and described the nichrome igniters. "These wires are the same as those in a toaster," he said, "and get very hot." He explained how this heat ignites the first stage, which sets off the second, and finally, the payload engines. He drew a diagram of the wires that led from the ignition control panel to the alligator lead clips and the terminals. "Then you plug the control panel to the battery, throw the switch, complete the circuit—and swoosh! A launch." The class clapped and Craig sat down.

Next Johnny held up a drawing of an engine. "The outside is paper casing," he said. "Inside is a solid propellant with a dual-thrust-level design. At the very tip is a ceramic nozzle into which the nichrome wires go, for easy ignition. This engine has a high initial thrust to stabilize the rocket quickly. That is, it has a large burning area, for faster consumption of fuel. After the first thrust, a delay-and-tracking-smoke charge goes off. This doesn't make the rocket go any faster but permits it to coast upward to its peak altitude. After that, an ejection charge goes off. This sets off the next rockets, or, if it's the last stage, it sets off the recovery system. In our case, we have a little parachute and a big one to bring the capsule down safely."

Mr. Brian asked Johnny to repeat what he had said. He went over it slowly. Then Mr. Brian added, "By the way, Mr. Smith says they're 'go.'" Everyone cheered.

Phil got up and drew a picture on the blackboard of the payload capsule with its recovery system. He showed where the transistor-transmitter was, and how the range finder would receive the signals from the transmitter and beep louder and louder the closer they came to the capsule. Craig sighed as he skipped the description of the test tube. When Phil finished, his shoulders pressed back and he seemed very tall.

Mr. Brian took over when Phil sat down. He leaned against the lab table and faced the class. "We need about four volunteers for the observation bunker," he said. The entire class of hands went up. He grinned. "In that case, I'll just take the officers of the science club. The rest will have to watch from shore." He turned to Steve. "What's the chance of getting your friend Officer Ricardo to relay the countdown through his car radio? If you borrowed one of the Police Department's portable transceivers you could set up a Batta to police car transmission so the students on the shore could follow the progress. As I visualize the situation, they can see most of the launch once it gets over the reeds."

Steve thought the policeman would help and said he would be responsible for setting it up. "We have our own small walkie-talkie system," he explained. "We'll use these to keep in touch with each other during the countdown." He

thought for a minute. "That'll make two systems. It's complicated, but we can do it."

Craig watched Mr. Brian page through his
notes. "I guess that's all," the teacher said. "See
you all Saturday." He turned to the four boys.
"Would you mind leaving your material with
me? I'd like to study it." Smiling happily they
stacked their folders on his desk.

But as Craig turned to leave he saw Johnny
slip out the drawings of the banner.

17 HOLDING AT
T-MINUS FOUR

The Friday of December 13 was the longest school day Craig had ever known. It dragged like a beaver's tail.

At last it was three o'clock. The first boys out were Steve, Phil, Craig, and Johnny in that order. They didn't wait for the bus, but ran ahead, piled their books on the upright piano at Craig's house, and burst in upon Mrs. Sutton at the kitchen telephone. She put her hand over the receiver and whispered to them, "Please be quiet, I'm talking to the director of the Board of Education." She glanced at Craig. "It's very important."

Craig guessed it was, though it seemed hard to believe in view of the day and the moment. He waited until she was finished.

"Can I spend the night at Batta?"

"Yes! Yes."

She went to the sink. Johnny dialed home and got permission, then Phil. He handed the phone to Steve, who hesitated, then smiled down on them from his extra inch of autumn growth. "I'll have dinner with you and set up the police transceiver in the command station. We'll check out the walkie-talkies, and then I'll come home. I have a date with Cathy. I'll bring Mr. Brian and the science club officers over in the morning."

Craig was not upset. He was beginning to accept Steve's idiocy. Furthermore, ever since September he had felt it was often more fun without Steve. Phil and Johnny and he could draw comic books and laugh at their own jokes, which Steve, he noticed, was not finding very amusing any more.

"It's okay," Craig said to Steve. "Who knows, I may even like a girl myself someday."

Phil shot Craig a dire look. Steve called

Officer Ricardo, who said he would bring the portable transceiver to the dock at five o'clock as well as the long-range police walkie-talkies.

Several hours later the sun set on its early December schedule, and the swamp buggy touched the island wharf. Craig heard the sentinel of a flock of crows call "Beware" to its fellows. The flock had apparently come to the protecting hemlocks on the island to roost for the night. They heeded their outpost's warning and departed as the boys came ashore with packs and radios. Feathers crackled as the birds flew.

Before supper Steve and Phil set up the communications system, and Craig and Johnny prepared the experimental snails. Then they went to Batta. Phil lit some charcoal he had brought in a bucket with holes punched around the bottom to give it oxygen, then set to work cooking hamburgers.

They ate dinner and talked. At seven they saw Steve off in the swamp buggy, ran back to Batta, switched on their lights, and slid into their sleeping bags. The water clock read seven-ten.

Phil rolled on his back and wondered how the science class would like the second-stage blast which had the powerful engines in it. He thought it would be glorious from the shore.

Craig said it would probably scare Cathy to death and they all laughed and agreed. Johnny hoped they had packed the banner right. Phil said they had, because he had folded it. As Craig thought about the banner his stomach whirled.

"That's gonna be a real surprise," Johnny said.

Craig nuzzled into his sheepskin bed. "You bet," he said.

After the movie Steve walked Cathy from the bus stop to her home. They climbed the winding road up the ridge holding hands as Steve explained the countdown.

He left Cathy at her door, not lingering to talk any more for he was anxious to be off. He started up the hill toward Mr. Brian's garage apartment, a made-over stable behind one of the big houses on the ridge. He had wanted to speak to him, but suddenly he did not. He went home.

However, in bed, his lights out, he found he could not sleep. Twice he got up and started downstairs to the telephone, and twice he went back.

At twelve-thirty he was still wide awake. He got up, bolted down the steps, and dialed Mr.

Brian's number before he changed his mind.

"I'm sorry to awaken you," he said when the teacher answered sleepily, "but I thought I'd better tell you something."

"What's the trouble?"

"I promised I wouldn't tell, but I think I oughta."

"Well, only if you want to."

"It's about the rocket." Pause. "In the payload is an experiment with snails. We didn't mention that in class."

Mr. Brian sounded relieved. "Good, what's it about?"

Steve told him briefly. "Good!" the teacher replied.

"That's not all I wanted to say." Pause. "When the first stage falls away a banner will be ejected on parachutes. We made this last fall when everyone was angry at us."

"Is it safe?"

"Oh, sure, it's just one of those things the engineering companies sell for thrills."

"So?"

"So, what's bothering me is what it says. I thought you ought to know since this is a class project now."

"Well?"

"Well, it says . . . and you gotta remember last fall when we were pretty disappointed in

everything . . . you know . . . no help from anybody . . ."

"Yes?"

"It says . . . 'Blast You All!' "

At first Mr. Brian laughed and Steve was relieved. Then he apparently thought about it
for he said, "Let's take it out if you're concerned."

"That's the trouble. We can't. That is, not
without the boys knowing I told. We all agreed
not to, so I can hardly take it out without my
losing my friends . . . and I'm something of a
turncoat in their eyes anyway . . . Cathy, and
dances, you know."

"Steve, don't worry about it. Maybe they'll
think you spelled 'Off' wrong and that it was
supposed to read 'Blast Off.' But don't worry.
Go to sleep."

"Okay. I guess it's not important. Maybe no
one'll care." He hung up and crawled back into
bed. Relieved, he fell asleep.

Batta Day began at five o'clock as the boys
at Batta ran outside to see how the day was
dawning. The stars were still out, the sky was
a cobalt blue. The homemade thermometer—
green ink in a Coke bottle, corked, with a straw
running into it—read thirty degrees. And the
sun was not even up. Craig held up a stick with

a cheesecloth butterfly net attached. It hung limp in the windless predawn.

"All's well," said Phil.

During breakfast Craig read off the Batta booster countdown once more; then they worked on the cork and buzzer in the water clock until eight. At that hour they decided to go out. The chickadees were gleaning the fat round hemlock cones, the air smelled of frost and dried catnip. Craig jumped on Johnny and rolled him to the ground. Johnny got a half nelson on Craig and pinned him. Phil watched. His rib was in no shape for wrestling.

At nine o'clock Craig heard the swamp buggy chugging across the slow stream. He grabbed Johnny and rushed to the wharf to greet Mr. Brian, Steve, and the officers of the science club. Mr. Brian called that the rest of the class was at the other wharf and that Officer Ricardo had his car all set. "Seems to be enjoying this," he added.

There were still things to do. Craig gave Mr. Brian a copy of the flight data and countdown sheets and watched him snap them on his clipboard. He was glad to see that the teacher was calm. He wasn't.

It was time to push back the rocket covering. Steve and Johnny leaned against its poles and gently shoved it away. The rocket pointed up into the sun and the clear blue sky.

"She's green all the way," Craig said to Mr. Brian. They both admired the cluster of first-stage rockets, the rounded cones, and the long slender second and third stages. The payload stood on the ground to the left, ready to be put in place at the count. The engines were in the supply box, laid out in order.

"I am terribly impressed," said Mr. Brian as he looked closely at the rocket.

At quarter to eleven Steve showed Mr. Brian and the two members of the club how to stand behind the mud bags in the observation bunker. Watches were wound and checked. Craig gave Mr. Brian a Batta walkie-talkie and showed him how to flip the buttons to listen or speak. He handed Phil and Steve theirs and kept the fourth. Johnny would be beside Steve in the command center and wouldn't need one.

Then Craig nudged Phil and they jumped to their posts in the launch pit. Steve sat beside Johnny on a stump in the command station. He checked the ignition control panel, then examined the police transceiver. He turned it on and opened the switch on the long-range walkie-talkie.

It sputtered, then a voice came over it. "KX2BAT unit two, this is KX2BAT unit one on Rushing Road. Come in Batta control. Do you read me? Over."

Steve answered into the transceiver so he would be amplified on the car radio. "All systems are go." He glanced through the observation window at Craig and Phil and looked at Johnny.

"It's green all the way," Steve added. A murmur arose in the walkie-talkie. Craig could hear the cheers of the class coming through. It sounded like a high wind. He grinned. There was a silence. Craig stared at his watch.

"It is now eleven A.M.," Steve went on. "The countdown for the Batta extracurricular activity will begin."

"T-minus twenty. Test communications systems."

Craig checked in, then Phil, Mr. Brian, and then Officer Ricardo on the police walkie-talkie.

"All systems are green," Steve announced.

"T-minus nineteen. Place engines in payload capsule assembly. Check fittings."

Craig worked swiftly. "Green and go," he said.

"T-minus eighteen. Check transistor payload beeper and radio direction finder system." Craig picked up the payload. Phil checked the radio direction finder.

"Hold," said Phil.

"Holding at T-minus eighteen for recheck of beep," Steve announced. Half a minute ticked off.

"Go!" Phil said.

"We are now resuming the count at T-minus seventeen. Check parachute recovery system for all stages including payload."

"Green."

"T-minus sixteen. Insert radio beeper into payload."

"Mission accomplished."

"T-minus fifteen. Check snails in test tube and seal."

"Accomplished."

"T-minus fourteen. Wrap aluminum insulation foil around test tube."

"Affirmative."

Carefully Steve leaned away from the transceiver so that his voice would be heard only on the Batta walkie-talkie.

"T-minus thirteen and one-half. Check banner assembly around second-stage booster."

"Hold!" It was Mr. Brian.

"We are holding at T-minus fourteen," Steve announced. He sounded puzzled.

Craig glanced up perplexed. Mr. Brian stepped into the launch pit. He picked up the payload, pulled off the lower capsule, and took out the aluminum-wrapped test tube. Craig stared, Phil scratched his head. They shrugged. Steve strained to see what he'd done, but the teacher's back was to him. Mr. Brian climbed from the pit and returned to the observation bunker.

"Proceed with countdown, Batta control," the teacher said.

"We are resuming the count at T-minus thirteen," Steve relayed. "Install payload capsule assembly on main booster."

"Mission accomplished."

"T-minus twelve. Install first- and second-stage booster engines."

"Accomplished."

"T-minus eleven. Install nichrome igniter wires in first-stage booster engines."

"Go."

"T-minus ten. Clean and attach microclips."

"Green and go."

"T-minus nine. Check firing angle."

"On the line."

"T-minus eight. Clear the area. Check for low-flying aircraft."

There was a sound from the shore. Craig imagined the class looking into the sky. They're either getting terribly noisy, he thought, or the communications system's going bad.

"Clear and go," said Mr. Brian, who had the widest view of the sky.

"T-minus seven. Recovery crew go to your stations!"

Phil and Craig plunged out of the pit, taking the radio direction finder and the Batta walkie-talkie with them. They skidded around the bushes and leaped onto the swamp buggy. Craig started the motor after two pulls, but did not put the engine in gear. Phil untied the line. He lifted his walkie-talkie.

"Ready and waiting."

"T-minus six. Arm the launch panel!" Johnny put his hand on the switch.

"Go," said Johnny.

"T-minus five."

"T-minus four." The police walkie-talkie crackled with a welling sound. Then it bellowed and thundered.

"Hold," Steve said. "We are holding at T-minus four for a communications check. Batta command to Officer Ricardo, we are getting a noisy reception. Do you read me clear?"

"I read you fine. The noise is your audience. There must be five hundred people here. There are cars on both side of the road holding up traffic. The whole police force is here except Harry, who stayed on fire duty. The town board is here. There are merchants, teachers, and newsmen. Over."

"Gee whizz!" said Steve.

"Furthermore," Officer Ricardo blared on, "Mr. Brundage has most of his congregation out and three buses have brought students from the Wilbur Junior High in Greensburg.

"Your parents are all here. They look nine feet tall. We're all with you. We hope it's 'Go' all the way!"

The crew on the island peered at each other over and around the mud bags. Phil and Craig on the swamp buggy whistled through their teeth.

"We are resuming the countdown at T-minus four.

"Three.

"Two.

"One.

"Zero.

"Ignition!" Johnny threw the switch. The engines fired instantly, held their power a few inches off the ground to steady the craft, then thundered into a fifty-mile-an-hour climb. "*We have a launch!*" Steve shouted. "We have a perfect launch!"

Craig saw the rocket rise above the edge of the pit. It sped over the tops of the reeds, going at twenty-five degrees to the vertical. It gleamed and the engines burned red. Smoke streamed out.

The class on shore shouted as it shot into

view and roared above the bushes, the trees, the top of the ridge.

"The first-stage engines have burnt out." Steve's voice was shaky. "There goes the first stage falling away!

"Whoops! The first-stage parachute has opened." Horns tooted.

A silence; the banner had dropped out of the parachute and fluttered open in the clear air. It rippled into view. "BLAS YOU ALL" it read as the T spiraled to earth.

Mr. Brian gasped over the Batta walkie-talkie.

"Bless you all, too!" shouted Mr. Brundage over the police walkie-talkie. "But learn to spell!"

The crowd laughed and cheered. "Ray! Ray! Hooray!"

Craig laughed and slapped Phil as the second stage ignited and the rocket sped on.

"The second stage has fallen away," Steve announced. "The third stage is ignited!" A red burst marked the explosion of the last engine.

"The payload engines have ignited!" Steve cried. The capsule shot higher and higher speeding upward now on its own momentum.

It reached its apogee, then arched over and began its descent.

"Two parachutes should open," Steve called

out, "bringing the payload capsule ten feet north by northeast of the far shore."

A small red parachute unfurled and blossomed. It was followed seconds later by a big striped one. Checked with a sudden jerk, the payload drifted earthward on the quiet morning air.

"Recovery crew!" Steve called. "The altiscope indicates it's coming down at splash point A. Take a fast ride!"

The grass mower engine roared and the awkward buggy rolled over the water.

"Phil to Steve. I hear the transmitter. It is beeping loud and clear. We are closing in on it. Man! It worked!"

Steve repeated Phil's message. Suddenly he shouted, "Phil caught it in the air! We have a perfect rescue. Now how 'bout that!"

Horns honked. Voices cheered. There were toots and whistles and a single blast on a trumpet.

"Unit one to unit two," Steve shouted in order to be heard over the roar. "We have a surprise for you. We have a surprise. Twelve snails have been sent up in the payload to see if they'll continue normal behavior at two thousand feet." Another sound arose from the shore, a bellow so loud it was heard above the communications system.

"Phil, can you give us any details?" Steve shouted. "Are the snails acting like they do in the swamp water? Raise your right hand if they are. Raise your left hand if there has been any change."

Phil and Craig lifted their heads simultaneously and stared at each other. "What's the matter with Steve?" Craig said.

"Is he crazy?" asked Phil.

"I dunno."

"Phil," Steve repeated, "raise your right hand if the snails are all right." The roar from the shore died as the audience waited. Suddenly Craig understood what had happened. He grabbed Phil's shoulder.

"The banner!" he said. "Mr. Brian found out about the banner, and I'll bet he thought he had taken it out! Steve doesn't know he took the snails!"

"My gosh, you're right," exclaimed Phil. "Now, whatda we say? We can't make him look stupid. He's too nice a guy. And *I* can't lie!"

Craig agreed as he thought of all the trouble Phil had gotten into in the first place by not telling the truth.

Phil bit his lip and leaned forward. "Here goes my neck," he said and lifted the walkie-talkie. Suddenly he gave a gasp of glee and reached into the water. He slowly raised his right hand.

"Aw, don't," Craig said. "It's not worth it."

"The snails are doing the same thing!" Phil announced firmly. Steve repeated his words. The crowd cheered. Horns blasted. Hands clapped.

Craig grabbed Phil's shoulder and shoved him back to search his face. "Whatdidja lie for?" he whispered. "You'll get it."

Phil held out a snail. "*This* snail is doing the same old thing," he chuckled. "No one asked me what snail." Craig sighed and slumped against the motor.

Phil clutched a paddle and steered the craft to shore. They were met by Steve, Johnny, the two students, and a tarrying Mr. Brian.

"Thanks, Phil!" Mr. Brian said as he came ashore. "But you didn't need to lie to cover for my stupidity."

"I didn't lie," said Phil with a huff. He handed Mr. Brian the snail he had found. "I've never seen a more normal snail in my life." Mr. Brian threw back his head and laughed from the bottom of his belly.

With a whoop Steve threw his arm around Phil. Craig whacked Steve on the back. Johnny jumped on Craig, he fell, and pulled Steve with him into the grass. The three rolled and wrestled. Phil held his chest and tried not to laugh for laughter hurt his rib; but he couldn't help it. So he laughed and then he cried and then he laughed again.

Horns resounded from the shore, voices rose and fell. Presently Officer Ricardo's voice boomed over the police walkie-talkie sitting unattended on the shelf of the command center.

"Bravo!" he crackled. Steve stumbled forward and picked up the instrument "——was great!" Officer Ricardo went on. "And by the way, the reporters here want to know what your next big project will be."

Craig paused in astonishment. After all the trouble they had been through, he thought the town couldn't possibly ask them to create more. Apparently all the boys felt the same, for Steve answered heavily, "College!"

Phil murmured, "High school!"

"The moon!" shouted Johnny desperately.

Craig rolled from his back to his belly and pressed his cheek into the orange-yellow grass. A raft of ducks gabbled beyond the island.

"The earth," he whispered, "the solid, solid earth."

About the Author

The enthusiastic reception that young people accord each new book by Jean George is warmly seconded by their parents, teachers, and librarians. Mrs. George is coauthor of *Dipper of Copper Creek*, which received the Aurianne Award for the most outstanding animal story published in 1957. *My Side of the Mountain, The Summer of the Falcon, Gull Number 737,* and *Spring Comes to the Ocean* all have affirmed her remarkable sensitivity both to the world of nature and to young people.

Mrs. George is a regular contributor of nature stories to *Reader's Digest.* She has held the position of art editor for *Pageant* magazine and has served as a newspaper reporter for the Washington *Post* and International News Service.

She lives in Chappaqua, New York, with her three children.